The Test

Amanda Linehan

Published by Amanda Linehan, 2019.

THE TEST
By Amanda Linehan

Copyright 2013 by Amanda Linehan

Edition: May 2019

Cover Design by Amanda Linehan

Cover Background Image: © Briancweed[1] | Dreamstime.com[2]

This book was previously published as *Dragon*.

---

1. https://www.dreamstime.com/briancweed_info

2. http://www.dreamstime.com/

CHAPTER 1

Silver pulled her car into the parking lot at school and put it in park. She sat there for a moment before opening the door and grabbing her bag off of the passenger seat. From here at least things seemed normal, but then again, she was still a little far from the entrance to the school.

She got out gingerly, her legs feeling wobbly as she placed them on the ground and lifted herself out of the seat.

Other students were walking to the building from their cars too, but she didn't recognize any of them as friends or acquaintances, which was good. The longer she could go before speaking to anyone the better.

Her legs walked forward and her head and torso followed behind them as she neared the side entrance.

She looked down at her hands once more, as she had already done dozens of times that morning, and checked them for any marks that would give her away. But she had scrubbed them clean trying to remove the dirt from the night before. She was pretty sure she had succeeded.

As she got closer to the doors, she saw exactly what she expected to see. There was a buzz, some kind of excitement. Students spoke hurriedly to each other, and their bodies moved with a quickness that made Silver think of insects flying over a rotting carcass. It wouldn't be long before she saw someone she knew.

"Silver!"

It was Jenna. A friend and fellow member of the cheerleading squad. Silver felt her breathing turn quick and shallow, and, just as her legs had taken over as she walked from the car, her voice now spoke of its own volition.

"Hey!" Silver said, trying to remember how she would normally greet one of her friends in the morning. She hoped she had gotten it right.

"Have you heard yet?" Jenna asked, looking thrilled to be the first person to tell Silver what had happened. "Somebody vandalized the school last night. The lobby is trashed!"

Silver knew her next move was to respond with surprise. She felt her breathing return to normal and her body start to feel whole again, as she got into character.

"Wait, what? Do they know who did it?"

"See for yourself. They're not letting us into the lobby, of course, but we can get close."

Silver put a perplexed look on her face as she grabbed the door handle and pulled it open.

What greeted her when she walked inside was pure chaos.

The hallways were mobbed and it was loud. There were a few teachers and administrators who tried to move people along, get them into their classrooms, but they were outnumbered by the agitated student body.

Silver and Jenna squeezed their way through the crowds and made a right into another hallway. This one was even worse. It ended at the lobby.

Silver was desperate to make it through to the end. To see the destruction in the full light of day. She pushed through the crowd, creating a path behind her for Jenna to follow. Finally, she was at the end.

As Jenna had said, the lobby was indeed trashed. Graffiti covered the walls. Trash cans were turned over, trophy and awards cases smashed with the contents lying broken on the floor. All ways into the lobby—the front doors and both of the hallways that led away from it—were roped off.

"Crazy, isn't it?" Jenna said, her eyes wide with excitement.

Out of the corner of her eye, Silver saw Mike with a group of three guys from the basketball team. He was looking around and making loud comments just like the rest of the students.

Silver looked around again just as Dave approached from the other hallway. He quietly approached the lobby to see what had happened. He was alone and didn't join one of the groups of on-lookers to discuss what had happened. Just as quickly as he appeared, he turned and left, apparently not interested enough to stick around.

"So what happened? Does anyone know anything about this?" Silver asked Jenna.

"I have no idea. I just got here about five minutes ago myself."

Silver wondered how far behind Anthony, her brother, was. Normally, they would have driven to school together. But today was different.

There was still twenty minutes before classes started. She felt someone push into her on her left side and looked over. It was Karly. She wanted to talk to her, but that might seem strange. She couldn't risk it. After a moment, Karly turned around and was swallowed by the crowd as she walked back the other way.

The level of energy in the room was high, yet Silver felt oddly disconnected from it all, as if she was a ghost floating by, observing this room full of humans and their emotions.

Silver looked down at her feet and saw a golden girl that had been severed from the top of a trophy. She picked it up and looked at it, the figure stiff in her hands, then squeezed her fist around it, feeling its edges dig into her palm.

A second later she felt better as she saw Anthony appear from the other hallway, towering above most of the other students. She waved at him through the crowd, standing on her tiptoes to get his attention. He finally spotted her and waved back, an expression on his face most would read as surprise, but in which she could spot fear.

Silver was starting to feel nervous again. She wasn't sure how she was going to make it through the day, but she knew if she did she would feel better, and knew that the more days she could put between herself and this morning, the better off she would be.

Just then it got louder throughout the lobby, and Silver realized that several police officers were coming through the door.

That was all she needed to see.

She turned back around, grabbing Jenna by the wrist, and made her way back down the hallway. It was time to go to class. His class.

Jenna said good-bye and scurried away, leaving Silver alone with the golden girl still in her hand. Silver looked at it for a moment and the marks the trophy top had left in her hand. She had the sudden urge to keep it, to put the golden girl into her bag, but in the end she spotted a trash can and tossed it away, a flash of gold disappearing into the abyss.

CHAPTER 2

Two Weeks and One Day Prior

Mr. Bailey carefully laid the paper down on Silver's desk as he strode through the rows with a stack of papers in hand. The entire class was quiet and anxious as they waited the results of their mid-term paper.

It was the same way every time they received an assignment or exam back. Mr. Bailey didn't just throw them all onto a desk and tell them to come up and get theirs. Nor did he sit at the front of the classroom calling out names and placing the papers in the hands that reached out to him. No.

He personally walked down the four rows of desks and handed the papers back one by one.

He would arrange them beforehand in the order that the students sat. They had assigned seats in Mr. Bailey's class, which was odd as almost all of them were seniors. But here in this class there was order. And a part of that order was that everyone should sit in the same seat every class.

Silver sat three desks from the front in the second row, so she had her paper before half the class did.

She stared at it for a moment without moving, leaning back against her chair and not picking it up. It was the thickest paper she had ever turned in during her tenure in high school. She had worked hard on it.

She didn't have to search for her grade. She could see it even while leaning back, not having touched a thing.

Blue ink. Mr. Bailey always graded in blue ink. It was a nice change from red, which despite standing out well, was harsh. But, Mr. Bailey always chose blue.

Out of the corner of her eye, she could see other students holding up their papers and flipping through them. A few people were already comparing things that Mr. Bailey had written. Some looked pleased with themselves. Some looked dejected.

Silver had no discernible expression on her face.

Since she was smart and had great grades and that was generally known, the fact that she wasn't making much of a fuss about her grade seemed normal. She probably had gotten an A.

But that wasn't the letter in blue ink that sat atop her paper. No, that letter was a B.

Normally, Silver wouldn't have sweated a B so much, as she would be pretty confident that she could make up for it with other assignments to have an overall grade of A.

But this was a big assignment, and not only that, but she had been having a more difficult time in this class than was usual for her.

Generally, in all her classes without exception, she could expect an A with little to moderate effort depending on the teacher and the subject. She was used to coasting by with little to no stress. It had been wonderful, and she had taken it for granted.

For the other three assignments in this class, she had grades of B, A, and B. Unfortunately, the A was on the smallest assignment and carried the least weight in her overall grade. She didn't have to be a math genius to know that three Bs and an A would not be an A overall.

She didn't want to shift in her seat because she knew as soon as she did, she would be able to feel the butterflies in her stomach.

She had been ignoring her growing anxiety about this class, but after this grade she couldn't avoid it any longer.

She would be submitting her college applications soon, and an overall grade of B in Advanced English didn't fit into her plan.

Silver wanted to attend one of the most selective universities in the nation. She thought there was a decent chance she could be accepted, but she knew without a perfect grade point average she had no chance.

She had been plotting her acceptance into this particular college since the beginning of high school, and knew that grades and standardized test scores were just the basics. She also planned out her extracurricular activities, making sure to demonstrate her leadership skills, commitment to service, and unique qualities, abilities, and interests.

Besides maintaining a perfect grade point average, her standardized test scores were excellent—not perfect, but excellent. She wasn't too worried about the fact that they weren't perfect, as some universities were beginning to give them less weight in the application package. She was captain of the cheerleading squad and student body president. Those things were good but not nearly enough.

In her quest, she had taken trips to foreign countries to serve local populations. She had founded and organized the "Service Club" at school to match students with volunteer opportunities, and she was doing everything she could to become fluent in Spanish, meeting once a week for coffee with a native speaker to increase her fluency.

She had courted awards and honor societies, and even served on the leadership boards of some. Her freshman year she had considered joining the marching band and learning to play the oboe to demonstrate an interest in the arts, but couldn't bring herself to do it. It would have been social suicide.

She did, however, try out for the school play, and actually got a small part, despite the fact that she had no acting experience and had no interest in it. She gritted her teeth and got through it, knowing that it would round out her resume.

Silver tried to give herself every edge she could think of for getting accepted to her first choice university. There was almost nothing she wouldn't do for her resume, and now, it seemed that English was finally going to break her.

Finally, Silver leaned forward in her seat and picked up her graded paper, accepting the inevitable. She flipped through it but barely read the comments in the margins. Only one thing mattered, and it was that letter at the top of the first page. The letter she didn't want.

She started to fidget as the anxiety spread through her body. Her left heel tapped the ground, and she drummed her fingers against the desk. She succeeded at most things she tried, and had such well-laid plans for her life that she was rarely caught off guard. She didn't quite know what to do.

She happened to look up and catch the grade on the paper of the guy who sat to her right and up one desk. An A. She knew his name was Dave and that he was a senior, but didn't know much else about him. This was a little odd as they had been going to school together since the sixth grade. But she didn't think anyone else knew much about him either.

He didn't talk much, and when he did, she figured it was probably to discuss role-playing games and fantasy novels. She was embarrassed just to know what those were. As far as she could tell, he wore the same denim jacket every day of his life, no matter the season. And even worse, he had hand drawn a picture of an elaborate dragon on the back of the jacket in black marker, which stood out against the worn denim and juxtaposed its utilitarian nature in a strange way.

To be honest, the drawing was kind of cool, but Silver found no rational excuse for why it should be on the back of a jean jacket. She had the vague impression that Dave was a good artist in general, but couldn't remember why she knew that. Also, she couldn't think of anyone—even in the weird crowd—who she knew to be his friend. For just a split second, she was struck by how lonely that must be, and then her empathy was overpowered by her growing anger.

What had he done in his paper that she hadn't been able to do? She didn't know him by reputation as being that smart, and she had trouble believing that he had outdone her. But it was true. The blue ink didn't lie.

Dave flipped through his paper carefully, actually taking the time to read the comments that Mr. Bailey had written. When he was done, Silver watched him slip his paper into his bag that was beside him on the floor, and pull out a heavily dog-eared paperback novel. He leaned back against his chair and began reading as Mr. Bailey started taking questions from the class about the grading and explained some common missteps within many of the papers. Dave apparently had no reason to listen. This really pissed her off.

She was now silently seething in her seat, the fluttery anxiety of a few moments prior had been replaced with heat that made its way slowly but surely up to her face, where she could feel her cheeks flush. Her skin tone concealed most of it, and she was glad for that.

"Hey," someone whispered on her left-hand side. It was Mike. He sat in the desk right next to her. "How did you do?" He flashed his paper at her showing her that he had received a B also.

She was slightly relieved that someone she knew had gotten the same grade, but just for a second. It didn't change the fact that this was not the grade she wanted.

To be nice, she flashed her paper back at him showing him her grade.

He nodded at her and smiled a conciliatory smile, knowing that she probably wanted the A. The gesture actually made her smile back at him.

Mike was one of the nicest and friendliest people that she knew, and she tried not to hold that against him. He had been friends with her brother since middle school, and she often saw him in social situations, including at her own house when Anthony had friends over. He was a great athlete, with a body so strong and lithe he made the most complicated movements look easy. At 6'0", with a well-toned, but not overly muscular, body, he excelled at both football and basketball, but would play neither competitively in college. Silver knew he had his sights set on medical school after college, and he would focus on that. Getting a B in English wouldn't set him back too much.

"Damn," Mike said, exaggerating the word a little bit, "what do you have to do to get an A on an assignment in this class?"

"Ask him," Silver said as she nodded her head in Dave's direction.

Mike raised both of his eyebrows in response to this, as if to ask "Really?" Silver nodded back. But not even Mike knew Dave enough to speak to him, and Dave was still lost in his book anyway.

Silver was not a reader herself, not for enjoyment anyway, and she never understood how people could read for extended periods of time when they didn't have to. Reading was for school, and hopefully had a purpose to it, like finding out an answer for an exam question. Otherwise, Silver felt no need to do it. Maybe it was something about sitting alone for long periods of time.

Mr. Bailey was still talking away, answering someone's question about a part of the paper. Silver hadn't heard what the question was because she had been talking to Mike, but truthfully she didn't care anyway. Mr. Bailey didn't allow resubmissions of assignments, so it wasn't like she could fix her paper and turn it in again. Her grade would stand.

Mike then turned around in his seat to the girl behind him.

"Hey, Karly," Mike said, "what did you get?"

The girl looked at him with a friendly expression, which turned sour when she said, "C plus."

"Well, hey," Mike said while flashing his signature smile, "at least you got that plus." He put his hand up to give her a high five, and as their palms touched, she smiled back at him, the dozen or so bracelets on her arm dangling and clinking together.

"What did you get?" she said.

"B," he said, still smiling.

"Not bad," Karly said. "Did anyone get an A?" She made an attempt to look around at some of the papers near her, but didn't see any.

"Silver said Dave did."

"Dave got an A? Damn!" Karly slammed her hands down on the desk in mock frustration as Mike quietly laughed.

Silver, who had been on the periphery of their conversation, made eye contact with Karly, who looked back at her.

Silver didn't know her well, and she didn't run in the same so-cial circles that she and Mike did. The fact that Mike knew her wasn't that surprising; he was friendly with practically everybody. Silver thought that she was new to the school sometime in the last couple of years. Silver only knew her as the girl-who-wore-all-that-jewelry.

Karly always had a few necklaces draped around her, bracelets up and down her arms, rings on seven of her ten fingers, and large earrings that you could see on the other end of the hallway if you wanted to.

Silver suddenly got the urge to look to her right, and found that Anthony was trying to get her attention. He sat all the way on the far right in the middle of the row. He was making hand signals to her that Silver finally realized meant he had gotten a C plus on the paper. He must have caught Mike's eye too, because he made the signal again and then fist pumped a couple of times while smiling.

Anthony was already committed to play basketball at a small, private college about two hours away from their home. He was hap-py just to pass everything at this point. Not that he wasn't smart, he just didn't feel like putting forth the effort now that he already had his college plans figured out.

She signed back to him that she had gotten a B, and his expres-sion dropped a bit at the news.

"Okay, that's it for today. See you folks tomorrow," Mr. Bailey said, as they could hear the sounds of the hallway coming alive, meaning that it was time to change classes. A couple seconds later the bell rang.

They all got up and grabbed their bags causing a cacophony of chairs and desks scraping against the floor. Mike was right behind

Silver as she walked out the door. When they entered the hallway, she turned to him so that he was on her left side.

"So how do you know her?" she asked.

"Who?" Mike said.

"Karly. That's her name, right?"

"Oh, we have ceramics together."

"You take ceramics?" Silver asked.

"Yeah, it's fun. Plus, my other three classes are English, Calculus, and Physics. I've got to do something that gives me a break during the day."

Their high school ran on a block schedule. The academic year was divided into two semesters where each student had four different classes, as opposed to the typical seven or eight that ran the entire year.

"How does your father feel about that?" Silver asked, teasing.

"Well, he agreed to it," Mike said with a smile that seemed hard to maintain. "He would have preferred something like Strength Training for an easy class. Something that would help for football and basketball, but I wanted to do something creative, so ceramics it was."

Silver noticed the strain in Mike's voice and movements, like he was pushing against some force that held him back. His father was well liked in the community, including by Silver, but she knew he held Mike to the highest standards. Mike met those standards, but she realized that must be exhausting sometimes.

"Is that where you're going now?" Silver asked.

"Yeah," Mike said, his usual enthusiasm having risen again. "Hey, remind me to show you what I'm working on sometime. It's this huge bowl, I actually did it all on the potter's wheel."

"All right," Silver said, feeling more amused with Mike than she normally did, "definitely show me sometime."

With that, he slung an arm around her shoulders and gave her a quick squeeze, flashed a smile at her, and then jogged off down the hallway toward the ceramics studio. She watched him wave to or greet at least three people before he was out of sight.

Silver had Psychology next, which was good as this wasn't as intellectually taxing as Advanced English (of course, nothing was as intellectually taxing as Advanced English). In fact, she currently had a 99 percent in this class, which gave her plenty of room to make a couple of mistakes while still earning an A.

She entered her classroom and sat down at the desk she usually sat in. No assigned seats in this class. Up on the board, her teacher had drawn a pyramid with five different levels, all labeled and with different colors for each level. Silver glanced at this with curiosity before her mind wandered back to English again. The butterflies returned to her stomach.

She didn't know what she was going to do. She had gotten temporarily distracted from this problem while talking to Mike, but now it was back in full force.

This would ruin everything. She had to figure out how to get an A in this class. But mathematically it might not be possible. Her heartbeat rose just at this thought.

She could try talking to Mr. Bailey about her grade, possibly getting her grade on the mid-term paper changed or maybe even negotiating a redo. But she knew that wouldn't work; he wasn't the type of teacher that students tried that on.

That left only the assignments going forward.

One of which, and the most important, was Mr. Bailey's legendary final exam. It was an all essay exam, and it was timed.

Everyone who stepped foot into Advanced English knew from the beginning of the semester what that exam would consist of, because Mr. Bailey never changed the structure of it from year to year, only the specific questions asked.

The exam would consist of seven essay questions, of which each student would pick five to answer, and would cover a variety of topics from the entire semester. However, the exam was only fifty minutes long (not ninety minutes like a regular class period), meaning that you had, on average, ten minutes to complete each question.

Silver needed an A on this exam if there was any chance of her receiving an A in the class, but considering what her performance had been thus far, she didn't know how she was going to pull it off. She had no problem working her ass off if she believed that would get her the grade, but she wasn't convinced.

Her other option was to cheat.

From what she had heard about the exam, this was almost impossible. For starters, it wasn't like she could just look at someone else's paper while taking the exam since the questions were essays. That was risky anyway. Also, she wasn't sure if everybody got the same seven questions, or if Mr. Bailey actually alternated exams. Silver made a mental note to figure that out.

The only way to cheat would be to get a copy of the exam ahead of time and memorize the questions. Taking a peak at the answers wouldn't hurt either, if there was such a document. Silver wasn't sure.

She needed an edge with this exam, she just wasn't sure how to get it.

CHAPTER 3

The next morning Silver sat down in her seat in the second row in English, and waited for Mr. Bailey to walk into the classroom and begin the lecture. The other students around her talked and joked with each other, even though it was first period and early in the morning. Silver, however, was still ruminating over her grade on the paper.

She sat quietly at her desk and looked out the window, which was on the other side of the room, and saw the morning sunlight touch the trees and parked cars outside.

It had bothered her all last night, the grade. In fact, she had even woken up a couple of times and it was the first thing on her mind, as it was this morning when she woke up. She had hoped that her subconscious would devise a plan while she slept and that in the morning it would all become clear to her what she was supposed to do. But it didn't. And in the morning she was just as stuck.

Anthony walked into the classroom, with just a minute to spare, and sat down in the seat in front of her which was unoccupied for the moment.

"What's with you this morning?" he said, forgoing a greeting.

She had bolted out of the car when they arrived, yelled a good-bye, and rushed up to school. It wasn't that she wanted or needed to get to school early, it was just that she wanted to move, or to do something. Even sitting here in this desk made her feel a little too constrained.

"What?" she asked, with the best annoyed tone she could come up with, as if nothing was wrong.

"You know what I mean. You practically ran from the car into the building."

"I can do whatever I want," Silver said as she crossed her arms in front of her.

"But what's up? Something's up. I know it. Is it your grade from yesterday?"

"Anthony, relax. I'm fine," Silver said a little more loudly than intended, as it drew a few looks from other students.

"All right," Anthony said, as he pulled his large frame out of the desk and walked to his side of the room, turning his back on her.

She sat there with her knee bobbing up and down, heel tapping the floor, and wasn't sure how she was going to sit through this class.

Just then, she saw a woman walk through the door and put her bag down by Mr. Bailey's desk. Silver realized it was actually a couple of minutes after 8:00 a.m.

"Hi, everyone, my name is Ms. Patton. Mr. Bailey is going to be out today, and I'm your substitute this morning. I apologize for being late; I only got the phone call an hour ago."

Silver was surprised. Mr. Bailey rarely missed school. In fact, he had some kind of streak going. Something like four and a half years since he had been absent. She had never paid much attention, always assuming he would be there, but now something about this struck her. She just wasn't sure why.

Then it hit her. Mr. Bailey was gone today, meaning he wouldn't be in his classroom at all, meaning she now had time and space in which to take a look around to see if she could find the upcoming exam.

Suddenly, Silver felt both energized and clearheaded. Her restlessness subsided, and she felt renewed. She had a plan, and now she would execute that plan.

"Yes? Do you have a question?"

Silver brought her attention back to the classroom and realized the substitute was talking to her.

"Oh, no ... no, I don't," Silver said.

"You looked like you got really excited there for a minute. I thought you might have something to say."

Silver smiled back at her and shook her head to confirm her answer. Out of the corner of her eye, she caught Anthony watching her, but as she turned her head toward him, his eyes went back toward the substitute.

"Okay, I guess we better get started," Silver heard Ms. Patton say as her thoughts turned back to her new opportunity.

The cheerleaders were meeting that afternoon after school to make banners and posters for the first home basketball game tomorrow. Depending on how many people were around, she could pop in before or after, or maybe even during, if she could come up with an excuse to get away for a while.

It was a long shot. There was a good chance the exam questions weren't in this room at all, but right now it was her best opportunity. Mr. Bailey was rarely absent, and now on the day after receiving her mid-term paper grade, he had finally missed a day of school. It was a sign, and Silver was sure of that. She would play it by ear this afternoon, and figure out the best time to come in and take a look around.

She realized that Ms. Patton had begun lecturing on something and she was blatantly not taking any notes. She reached down to her bag to grab a pen and a notebook, but as she did, the pen popped out of her hands and rolled over to her right and next to a fantasy novel that had been placed on the ground.

Dave looked down as he heard it drop, and saw it roll right by his stuff. He bent down to pick it up, then leaned over to Silver holding her pen out to her.

They made eye contact, and Silver felt awkward, a rare emotion for her.

"Thanks," she said.

"No problem," Dave said, as he turned back around in his seat, the dragon on the back of his jacket glaring at her.

* * *

"Silver! We need some red. Where's the red spray paint?" Nicole called out as Silver walked up from her car to where the cheerleaders had stationed themselves outside to make the banners and decorations for tomorrow's basketball game.

Silver looked at the cans in the bag she was carrying, and didn't see any red.

"I don't have it. You guys must already have it with you."

"There's no red paint up here at all."

Silver finally reached the other cheerleaders, and set down the bag she had been carrying. She looked through it again and this time she saw the red paint.

"Here you go," Silver said as she handed the can to Nicole, who immediately shook it up, the can clanking as she did so, and depressed the button on top to release a stream of red paint.

They had decided to use spray paint for all the decorations, mostly because it was easier to do large banners that way, but also because it gave it a graffiti-look that was kind of cool.

Also, they were giving each basketball player a plastic spear to run out with, as the school's mascot was the Warriors. The spears would be painted gold because right now they looked like little kids' toys, which they actually were.

Silver thought the golden spears were a little dramatic, but it had been Nicole's idea and she was really into it. Silver decided just to go along with it.

"Dammit," said Matt, one of two male cheerleaders on the squad, "I just got gold paint on the sidewalk."

"No use crying over spilt milk," Silver said. "Just try not to let it happen again. We don't want the administration all over us for graffiti-ing the sidewalk."

"I'm sure you'd charm us right out of trouble," Matt said, giving Silver a grin. She just chuckled.

There were two guys on the cheerleading squad: Matt and Rob. Both of them strong, stocky guys who could throw around the smaller girls on the squad like whiffle balls.

Silver couldn't figure out why a guy would want to be on the cheerleading squad, but everyone got along well and they both seemed to enjoy it. And, it was an advantage to have that strength, so Silver saw it as a win-win.

She hadn't been able to look around in Mr. Bailey's classroom before they had started painting. She had walked by the room fifteen minutes or so after classes had ended, but there were still too many people around for her liking, although the substitute had left. The good news was that the door was left open. She had feared that it might be locked, but that didn't look to be the case.

She hadn't yet come up with a good excuse to get away from the painting and take a look around, but she knew she could always go by after they were finished. But it was killing her to wait; it was all she could think about.

"I'm so sorry!" Silver heard a female voice call out to her left. She looked over and saw Ashley with her hands over her mouth and eyes wide in apology. Rob stood in front of her with a patch of red spray paint on his gray sweatpants.

"You do know that I will be throwing you into the air tomorrow night, right?" Rob said.

All of the squad had now turned to look and laughter rippled through them as they all stared at Rob's predicament.

"I didn't mean to. I'm sorry," Ashley said again as she tried to hide a giggle.

Rob sighed and shook his head at her, as she proceeded to throw her tiny body at his thick frame for a hug. He finally put his arms around her and hugged her back.

Silver made a mental note not to use spray paint again. At this rate, all of them and the sidewalks would be covered.

All of a sudden, she had an idea.

"Hey, guys, I'm going to change clothes. I'll be back in a few minutes."

"I'll go with you," Nicole said, "I don't want to end up looking like one of those spears."

"No!" Silver said just a little too loudly. Nicole looked at her perplexed, and a little startled. "You stay here and supervise," Silver gave her a look, "and I'll grab your stuff from your locker."

"Okay," Nicole said, "it's the black sweatpants we got freshman year, and I think there's a T-shirt in there too."

"Got it," Silver said, as she began walking toward the doors to the school.

She knew that the opportunity she needed would come up, she only had to recognize it. This would definitely give her time to look around thoroughly, especially since she now had to get Nicole's clothes. Nicole's request had actually played into her favor.

It was quiet inside the school. Peaceful, but strange given that she normally walked these hallways when they were packed with students. She realized that she was walking so as not to make a lot of noise, and then realized that there was no need to do that since there was no one around. Even if she came upon somebody, it wouldn't be a problem. She was here with the cheerleaders after school and she was just getting some clothes from her locker. They were having trouble keeping the paint on the banners, she would say, chuckling as the other person laughed too. They would then pass her by without another thought, which was fine by Silver.

She had yet to see a soul, and she was already at Mr. Bailey's classroom. Door ajar, lights off, the lessening afternoon sun through the windows providing just enough light to see by.

Silver hesitated for a moment as she asked herself what she would do if someone saw her looking around in here, and then decided that she would figure out something to say. It would come to her, she knew it.

She pushed the door open wider and slipped into the still classroom.

She tried the most obvious place first. Opening his desk drawers quickly, she rummaged through the contents as thoroughly as she could. She sort of hoped she might find something scandalous but she saw nothing of the sort. She did, however, notice a memo that was dated October 20, 1989. She wasn't even born yet, clearly he wasn't cleaning this out on a regular basis. She moved on.

Silver looked around the room, feeling like a predator looking for her dinner. Her eyes darted to all the possible places she might check.

Her eyes locked on the file cabinets and she started in on them. These could very well be locked but she was going to try all of them as fast as she possibly could.

A noise outside the classroom door startled her for a moment. She stopped, standing very still, her ears listening for the slightest sound. She thought she heard a sneaker squeak on the floor, but as she listened carefully all she heard was the silence, which she thought was loud enough. Satisfied, she turned back to the file cabinets.

She knew right away she wasn't going to find the exams here. The cabinets were filled with old papers, many from the eighties and some even from the seventies. She half expected to find her parents' names on one or two of these papers. There was nothing new kept here, these were just storage. Although, she couldn't figure out why he kept this stuff around. If it had been her, she would have thrown all this stuff in a pile outside and torched it. No need to keep around a bunch of paper in this day and age.

Although she had resigned herself to the fact that she wasn't going to find the exam or the answers, Silver looked through each and every drawer in every cabinet, holding out for the slightest possibility that they were here. She wasn't going to waste the opportunity she had been given, even though it appeared that it wouldn't be fruitful.

Finally, she finished checking the last drawer and shut it. She stood for a moment in the middle of the classroom looking around and trying to see if there were any other places to check, but she had covered them all. It was time to head back to the other cheerleaders anyway.

"What are you doing in there?"

Silver jumped and let out a shriek that she hoped no one had heard. Well, no one except the person who was leaning in the doorway looking at her.

It was Dave.

"Oh my God, you scared me," Silver said, her hand over her heart and her breathing heavy. "Do you always go around sneaking up on people?"

"Do you always spend your afternoons snooping through classrooms?" Dave asked, his arms crossed in front of him and a smile on his face.

"I wasn't snooping," Silver said, as she started to calm down, "I left my copy of *The Stranger* somewhere. I came to see if I had left it here."

That was good. She knew that she would think of something. She looked back at Dave as if to dare him to challenge her on this one.

"So you think you might have left it in one of the file cabinets?"

Shit. He had seen her.

"You've been watching me," Silver said as she felt her face starting to flush.

"You've been snooping through someone else's stuff."

Dave was clearly enjoying this, and Silver knew that he had her in a difficult position. She decided that conceding was her best option.

"All right, you caught me. I was snooping around." She sat back against one of the desks nearby and crossed her arms over her chest. Her anger was mounting as she felt herself trapped.

Dave didn't respond immediately. He looked at her, almost as if he was trying to see something that she wasn't telling him. He had not moved from his position in the doorway. Suddenly, his smile grew larger.

"You're trying to find the final exam questions and answers, aren't you?" He started laughing, a big, hearty laugh that Silver hoped wouldn't draw any more attention to this classroom.

"Shhhh!" Silver said, waving her hands at him to get him to stop. "Are you crazy? Someone's going to hear us in here."

"This doesn't have anything to do with me," Dave said, still chuckling. "I'm not the one looking through all the file cabinets. I bet you looked through his desk, too."

Silver was grateful at this last comment, because it meant he hadn't actually seen her looking through the desk drawers.

"So?" Dave asked.

"So, what?" Silver said.

"So, were you looking for the final exam?"

He could see the answer on her face, she knew he could, so she just told the truth.

"Yeah."

She could see that he was a little surprised that she was being so blunt with him, but also happy he was right.

"You know he doesn't keep it here, right?"

"I know now," Silver said, starting to tire of the conversation. "Listen, you caught me, all right. I've got to get back to the other cheerleaders."

She began walking toward the door, but Dave didn't move.

"Can I get by, please?" She couldn't believe that she was being so polite.

"But you're smart," Dave said, not having moved a muscle. He wasn't exactly muscular, but he was stocky, and, frankly, Silver had never realized how big he actually was. He wasn't as tall as her brother, or Mike, but almost.

"Yes, I am smart."

"Then why do you need to cheat on the final exam?"

He was still looking at her as if she were a specimen under a microscope, trying to figure her out. His eyes bore through her, as if he could see into her body and straight to her soul.

"Because I need an A in this class."

"What do you have now?"

"I have a B."

He made a noise like someone twisting the cap off a bottle of soda.

"You have a B in this class, but you still want to take the risk to cheat on the final exam?"

"I need it," Silver said, her voice rising not only out of anger, but out of the desperation that had been lurking just beneath the surface since she had received her mid-term paper grade.

Dave just rolled his eyes.

"If I had everything that you have, I don't think there would be anything in the world that I could possibly need." He said this without smiling at all.

Now Silver was angry.

"Frankly, it's none of your goddamn business what I need or why I need it, and now, if you don't mind, I'd like to get by."

They stared at each other for a few seconds, neither of them backing down. Finally, Dave stepped aside and motioned with his arm for her to pass by him, exaggerating the courtesy.

Silver walked through the doorway and looked back at Dave to give him one last dirty look, then turned and walked down the hallway.

"Oh, by the way," Dave said, "the final exam and answer key are in his house."

Silver wanted to ignore him, to walk right down the hallway without giving him any more of her attention. But she stopped instead.

"In his house?" she asked.

"Yep," Dave said.

"Why would he keep it there?" Silver asked, trying to sound very casual.

"Well, I guess we both know that answer now, don't we?" Dave said, smiling again. "Honestly, I used to think he was really paranoid for doing that. Clearly I was wrong."

Silver hated that he was mocking her to her face, but she was in no position to defend herself now, something she would have already done swiftly in a different situation.

She rolled her eyes and turned back down the hallway once again. Then it hit her.

"Wait. How do you know that?" Silver asked, turning around to face Dave once more.

"He's my neighbor. Sometimes he has me come over and feed his cats while he's away, so I've been in his house before."

Silver had gotten the information she wanted but now didn't know what to do with it. She looked at Dave a moment.

He seemed disappointed that he had nothing more that she wanted.

"Anyways, you'd have to break into his house if you wanted to get those answers. And I'm pretty sure that felonies don't look that good on college applications."

Something inside of her felt satisfied with what she had received. She was ready to go.

"You going to tell anyone?" Silver was pretty sure she already knew the answer, she just wanted to make sure.

A strange look came over Dave's face, something Silver couldn't place.

"No, your secret's safe with me."

She gave him half a smile in return.

As she walked down the hallway for the second time, she heard Dave's footsteps heading in the opposite direction and was glad to be rid of him.

For some reason, she hadn't been too worried he would tell someone else what she had been doing. And, apparently, she had been right.

Of course, now he had something over her should he ever need anything from her. But what could he possibly try to get from her? Silver wasn't too worried. If he did try to blackmail her, it was her reputation versus his, and she knew which one would win.

Actually, he probably didn't realize how much power he now had. And Silver wasn't going to fill him in.

Her mind left this thought behind and she returned once more to the mission at hand. The one she had just failed.

Dammit, she thought. There were no exams or answer keys in that classroom. But at least now she knew.

Reality was starting to close in on her, making her footsteps down the hall heavy. She would get a B in English, and her grade point average would be ruined.

She felt tears fill her eyes as she got closer to the other cheerleaders, and she wiped one that had escaped from the corner with the back of her hand. She stopped so she could compose herself. She didn't want anyone to see her crying.

But suddenly, the composure she was trying to hold onto cracked and the tears that had filled her eyes spilled over the edge. Her throat tightened and she felt warm in the face. A few sobs escaped her mouth and finally she sat down on the floor and leaned back against the cool, concrete wall.

She laid her head back, as her eyes released the last bit of moisture they held.

What will I do? Silver kept thinking to herself as she imagined herself at one of the state universities, taking classes like some ordinary student. This wasn't how this was supposed to go. She wanted extraordinary. She wanted unique and special. And now, she would be just like everyone else. An above average person, but not the best.

No. It isn't supposed to happen this way. The signs were all there. Mr. Bailey being absent today for the first time in practically a thousand years. Having a meeting with the cheerleaders after school. Everything had led her to Mr. Bailey's classroom this afternoon. But she hadn't found what she was looking for. So, what was she supposed to find?

The tears had dried up. Her brain was working overtime, and, suddenly, Silver felt energized again.

"You'd have to break into his house if you wanted to get those answers."

That was it. She sat upright, her whole body buzzing with the hope that had filled her once more.

She would have to break in to Mr. Bailey's house. She just had to figure out how to do it.

* * *

"Where are my clothes? And why didn't you change? You were gone long enough to have driven home and back."

Damn. Silver had completely forgotten why she was supposed to be gone.

"Sorry," she said, trying to sound like there was a completely good reason for this. "I realized that I didn't have any other clothes with me today. I thought I did." She made a face like she was really annoyed at this, and Nicole seemed to buy it. "Then I ran into someone I know, and we got caught up talking, and, I'm sorry, I was practically outside before I remembered that I was supposed to get your clothes. But I figured that since I wasn't able to change you shouldn't be able to either, so I didn't turn around."

She gave Nicole a teasing smile that was as much apology as it was a joke.

"Fine," Nicole said in a long drawn out fashion. "At least I don't look like Rob."

"Why? What happened to—"

Silver never got to finish as Rob stood up from the spear he was working on, covered with spray paint marks.

"I had a few more accidents," Rob said, as he looked toward Ashley, who had just the faintest trace of a smile.

Silver looked back and forth at both of them.

"Next time I'm giving you all crayons."

CHAPTER 4

Silver lay awake early in the morning. At least two hours earlier than she had to get up for school.

The blackness in her bedroom was punctuated only by the blue light of her alarm clock. There must have been no moon that night.

She wasn't restless. There had been no tossing and turning. In fact, she had slept solidly for several hours. Then she had popped awake.

The thought was right there at the front of her consciousness.

"You'd have to break in ..."

It was the only way. Her last chance. She had to do it. She had to break into Mr. Bailey's house.

She knew this was an actual crime. Not just rule-breaking. If she had been caught snooping around his classroom that wouldn't have been pleasant, but it wouldn't be anything compared to getting caught breaking and entering.

But she didn't care. It was her last resort.

She needed to find help. Dave was her best bet, but that would be tricky. He wouldn't help her willingly. He would want something in return. But that was okay. She was sure that she could find something that he wanted.

Anthony. She knew she could get him to help her. That would be fairly easy.

But who else? Dave wasn't a definite, and just she and Anthony alone weren't going to cut it.

Mike. That was it. Mike was a good one, and he might fall easily if he knew Anthony was in. Unfortunately for her, however, he was an upstanding-citizen-type of person. He probably felt guilty speeding in his car.

Regardless, Silver had a good feeling about Mike. She would stick with this plan.

Anthony and Mike. But how would she bring this up? What would she say to them?

She looked at the clock. It was 4:44 a.m.

A sign.

She knew then that it would come to her. She would keep her eyes open for the opportunity to convince the two of them, and when she saw it she would jump on it. She'd think of something to say when the moment came. And she knew it would. She would figure out what to do about Dave later.

Her eyes began to feel heavy again, and without noticing it, her breathing fell to a slow rhythm. In a few minutes she was back asleep, her mind peaceful once more.

* * *

Later that morning at school, Silver was on high alert. It was as if all her senses had become ten times more sensitive than they were yesterday. She went through her morning classes keeping her eyes open for any sign that now was the time. But it hadn't come yet.

Not even in English, which she had with both Mike and Anthony. That might not have been the wisest move anyway, considering that Mr. Bailey taught the class.

She and Anthony had driven to school together that morning, and the entire time they were alone in the car together Silver kept waiting for the right moment. But it never came.

She sat through English and Psychology feeling like she might snap in two from the tension. The last few minutes of Psychology dragged by as she waited for the bell to ring, signaling her lunch period.

Finally, it was over and she walked to the cafeteria, making just a quick stop at her locker on the way.

She actually shared her lunch period with both Anthony and Mike, but she didn't think this would be a good time. Too many people around. Too loud. This called for finesse.

She entered the large room with the long tables and distinct smell of cafeteria prepared food, and to her surprise and delight, saw Mike and Anthony sitting together. Alone.

"Where are the other guys?" she asked, sitting down on the bench next to her brother.

The boys looked at each other and starting laughing.

"Detention," Anthony said through a full mouth, still laughing, little bits of food spraying the table. Mike continued to laugh also.

"Do I want to know?" Silver asked, already knowing the answer.

"No," they both answered in unison, still laughing. Finally Anthony composed himself.

"So what's up with you?" he asked.

"Nothing," she said, giving the default reply. She gave a little sigh afterwards. Nothing obvious. But something she knew Anthony would notice.

"What?" Anthony asked, the smile wiped clean from his face. His forehead wrinkled.

"Nothing," Silver said, as her voice rose a little higher in tone and she shrugged her shoulders.

"You're not still worried about the mid-term paper from English, are you?"

"No, not really ... well, I don't know ... I don't think I can get an A anymore in the class, so that kind of sucks."

She hadn't planned on doing this now, but the opportunity was clearly presenting itself. She decided to just go with it.

"But hardly anyone's getting an A in that class," Mike said, then reconsidered. "Well, maybe Dave is."

"You mean jean-jacket boy?" Anthony asked. "With the dragon? Man, that guy's weird. He was tutoring one of the guys on the team in something. Talked about elves the whole time."

"He reads a lot of fantasy novels, I think," Silver said, getting strange looks from both Mike and Anthony. "What? He practically sits right next to me. He's always pulling out a book."

"I don't care what he's reading. Elves are not an appropriate conversation topic," Anthony said, looking incredibly grateful that he never had the urge to talk about elves. "I mean, seriously, social suicide," he finished.

Silver suddenly remembered her objective, and sat quietly with an expression on her face that she hoped would make them feel guilty for turning the conversation away from her problem. It worked.

"So you can't get an A at all? What about all your plans?" Anthony asked, his forehead wrinkled again.

"Exactly," she said, hoping that her face looked sad enough.

"Well, can't you go talk to Mr. Bailey or something?" Anthony said.

"I thought about it, but I've heard he's not really the type for negotiations."

"Oh come on, Silver," Mike said, looking very serious, "I'm sure you could come up with something Mr. Bailey would negotiate for." Mike's mouth widened into a large grin, as he started making obscene gestures with his hands and body. Silver cocked her head to the side and pursed her lips.

"I do have some dignity, you know," Silver said, as she balled up a napkin and threw it at Mike.

"Yeah, emphasis on the *some*," Anthony said, while he and Mike laughed even harder.

"You know, I always thought that Mr. Bailey might be gay," Anthony said, his laughter subsiding.

"Well, in that case," Silver said, "you can do the negotiating, Mike."

Mike picked up the napkin she had thrown at him earlier and threw it back at her. Silver dodged it and it flew over her shoulder.

"No, seriously, I think he's divorced," Silver said, as the boys looked at her like they wanted more information. "From a woman," she finished. The boys appeared to accept this answer.

"You could always cheat," Anthony said, bringing the conversation back around to Silver's grade.

"I thought of that already. And it's pretty much impossible."

"Why is that?"

"We all know what that exam is like. I can't just copy someone's answers. I've got to have an answer key and that's not anywhere that I can find it."

"Why don't you sneak into his classroom and steal it?" Mike said, obviously making a joke.

"I already tried that," she said, dead serious. Mike looked taken aback.

"You did?" they both asked at the same time, looking incredulous.

"I was desperate," she said, a little too much emotion coming out in her voice. They both looked at her for a moment, an expression on their faces that Silver couldn't quite read.

"It's not in his classroom," Silver said, her tone of voice becoming serious after all the joking they had done.

"Where else could it be?" Anthony asked.

"He keeps the exam and the answer key in his house," she said.

"How do you know that?" Anthony asked.

"Um—" Silver started, but was cut off by Mike.

"Perfect," Mike said, "all we have to do is break in and steal them."

As both boys laughed at Mike's joke, they forgot all about where Silver had gotten her information. She couldn't believe how well this was all coming together. While Mike was enjoying the absurdity of his suggestion, he didn't realize he had suggested exactly what she wanted to do. Anthony picked up where Mike left off.

"Yeah, we could get those hats or whatever they are that go over your whole face, with just eye holes. And we could dress all in black. And get walkie-talkies or something to keep in contact with each other," Anthony said enthusiastically, enjoying his imagination.

"Nice!" Mike said. "We could pick a night when he's out, doing whatever it is he does, and get like a lock picking kit to get in through his back door or something."

"Oooh, or we could use a credit card or something. I saw that on TV," Anthony said.

"It'll be just like robbing a Vegas casino, except instead of a boatload of cash, we get one of the most valuable items at this school," Mike said.

"We can sell them!" Anthony said, the food on his tray long forgotten. "And we'll all get an A on the exam ourselves."

"If I was you, I would just go for the B," Mike said. "We don't want to make Mr. Bailey too suspicious."

At this both of the boys threw their heads back and laughed. Some other students turned around and looked at them.

"All right, it's decided then," Mike said, "we break into Mr. Bailey's house and steal the exams." He smiled widely, enjoying his session of make believe, not understanding what he had just done.

Silver had remained quiet through all this. Incredulous at the fact that the two boys had come to the exact conclusion she had wanted them to. Thinking it was a joke, of course, but to her it felt like this whole situation had fallen directly into her hands.

"You know," she said, taking a sip of her water, "if we really wanted to, it probably wouldn't be that hard."

Despite being in a loud cafeteria, suddenly it seemed as if the three of them were in their own bubble where it had just gotten silent.

"What do you mean?" Anthony said, just a trace of a smile left on his face.

"I mean, breaking into Mr. Bailey's house is probably doable." Silver said this without any trace of humor. "Dave is Mr. Bailey's neighbor. When Mr. Bailey's away, Dave feeds his cats, which means that he probably has a key to Mr. Bailey's house. We wouldn't even need to break in."

The boys stared at her. Not protesting, but not acquiescing either. Suddenly, Silver felt very powerful.

"Dave with the dragon?" Anthony said. Silver knew he was stalling. She would play along.

"Yep," she said, slightly enjoying the discomfort of the two boys.

"You talk to him?" Anthony asked.

"No. Well, I have. He caught me looking around Mr. Bailey's classroom."

"Silver!" Anthony said, looking worried again.

"I know, I know. It was after school and I didn't think anyone else was around," she said.

"He knows what you were looking for?"

"Yep."

"You told him?"

"He guessed and then I told him he was right."

"That's not good," Anthony said, shaking his head as his forehead wrinkled again.

"Anth, it's fine. Plus, we can't do this without him. He's a part of the plan."

"What plan?"

It was Mike. He had gone quiet since they had seriously starting talking about breaking in to Mr. Bailey's house. He sat sideways on the bench, his right forearm and elbow resting on the table. The look on his face was somewhere between disbelief and fascination. Silver knew she had him right where she wanted him.

"The plan to steal the exam from Mr. Bailey's house, of course."

She said this like they had been talking about it for weeks. Like they had simply decided on plans for the weekend.

"This is a crime," Mike said, his eyes growing wider.

Silver didn't feel like responding to that statement.

"Look, if we have a key to his house and we know that he's gone out—which we will because of Dave—we go in, take the exam, and leave. It takes us three minutes, we lock the door, and he has no idea that we've been in his house."

Mike looked at her like she had just grown an extra head. Anthony sat beside her, silent, listening.

"How many difficult classes do you have this semester?"

Mike held up three fingers.

"That's what I thought. So you have three hard classes to study for. And, I know you guys are playing the most difficult schedule the boys' basketball team has ever had. Wouldn't you like to know that you have the English exam wrapped up? That you don't have to do any work for it?"

Mike put his hand to his face and began running his fingers overs his lips. The resistance draining slowly from his face.

"If I were you, I'd want to limit the amount of work I had to do, but that's just me. And you," she looked at Anthony, "we all know you like to do the least amount of work possible at any point in the year. You'd pretty much be done with English."

This, Anthony couldn't argue with. His raised his eyebrows considering. "You're sure Dave can get us in and let us know when Mr. Bailey will be out?"

"Yes, absolutely," her face was stone. "Mike?"

Mike looked scared. She half-expected a bead of sweat to roll down his forehead at any second. His eyes were cast downward.

"My father would kill me," he said quietly. Silver wasn't sure whether he was speaking to them or to himself. She decided it was time to stick the sword in all the way to the hilt.

"What your father wants is for you to have the best grades and score at least twenty points every night."

Mike looked at both of them, and something innocent showed on his face. It made Silver hesitate for just a moment, wondering what she was getting them into. Then all doubt left her.

"If we get caught ..." Mike said.

"We won't," Silver said with all the certainty she could muster.

"Are you in?" Mike asked, looking at Anthony.

There was a moment of silence where Silver looked at Anthony, knowing that this whole operation rested on his answer.

"Yeah, I'm in. I'll take an easy B on an exam any day," he said, smiling widely, pushing the anxiety off his face. Mike smiled in return.

"It would be nice to take the easy way out this one time," he said, forcing himself to smile and relax.

"So it's settled then?" she said, not wanting to give them any time to back out.

The boys looked at each other, then looked at her and nodded.

"Okay," Silver was all business, "I've got to get Dave to agree to help us."

"How are you going to do that?" Anthony asked. "You're the only one of us that has ever spoken to him, and he's not exactly part of our crowd."

"I don't know," Silver said. "I'll figure something out."

Silver was slightly worried about this part, but she felt like she could do it. The only problem was that Dave was the one with something over her already, and now she was going to come to him again and ask for a favor. Usually, she wouldn't be so worried approaching any male for help, but for some reason she didn't see Dave as such an easy target. Something about him seemed tricky to her.

"Wait a minute," Mike said, suddenly looking relieved that there might be an out, "what's in this for Dave? We saw his paper, Silver, he had an A. I would assume his overall grade is the same."

Mike was right. She hadn't thought of this. She considered for a moment, and then decided that the plan was still worth executing.

"Everyone wants something. I just have to find out what Dave wants."

Mike just looked at her, some of the relief leaving his face. Anthony's forehead had wrinkled again.

"Anyway, I'll take care of Dave. You two just wait for instructions."

The boys just sat and looked at her, seeming a little stunned. Now that they had agreed, they didn't know what to say.

Silver couldn't believe her luck. She had seen the signs and followed them, and she had not been led astray. This had all been too easy. She would do the same thing in convincing Dave. She knew she could get him to agree. Everyone wanted something. Everyone. Even Dave.

It was just about time for her to return to class. Her objective had been fulfilled.

"All right, guys," Silver said, "I've got to go. Keep your ears open." She flashed them both a smile over her shoulder on the way out.

The last thing she saw was Mike and Anthony staring at each other, not saying a word, dazed expressions on their faces. The funny thing, Silver thought, is that they had been the ones to suggest it.

She walked out into the hallway and turned left, not paying any attention to the people around her. To her right, in the art case, something caught her eye.

A ceramic dragon, its wings outstretched and body slightly spiraled as if it were moving toward the sky.

It was a sign.

CHAPTER 5

School was over and the hallways were empty. Silver moved through them enjoying the stillness on her way out the door and to her car. Anthony was waiting for her there.

There was a basketball game tonight, so the two of them would go home for a bit and come back up to school in a couple hours to get ready to play and cheer.

Silver thought about her good luck at lunch today. Everything was falling into place. Her agitation from that morning had left her, and she now felt perfectly good.

She hadn't thought yet about how to approach Dave, but it wasn't time for that yet. She would think about it later.

She passed the art case she had seen earlier, and once again the spiraled dragon caught her eye.

She stopped this time to admire it, wishing she could touch it through the glass.

It was blue and green, with accents of silver giving it a reptilian, but also magical look. She wondered where it was going, where it would fly to if it could leave this case.

"Admiring my dragon, are you?"

She jumped, startled that someone was standing next to her. It was Dave.

Instead of excitement at the possible opportunity, anger spread through her body, hot and fast. She didn't like that he had snuck up on her like this. And she especially didn't like that he was the artist who had created the dragon.

"I see you're back to stalking me," Silver said, trying to hide her surprise, but letting her anger pour out.

"This isn't your private hallway. I'm allowed to walk down it, without accusations of stalking," Dave said, laughing a little. This made her even more angry.

"And I'm allowed to look in the art case without being accused of being a crazed fan of yours. I wasn't even looking at that dragon."

"Really," Dave said, looking smug, "I bet you can't even tell me what else is in the case. And I won't ask you to because I don't want to embarrass you."

Silver couldn't believe it. He was enjoying making her feel uncomfortable. And even though she wouldn't admit it, she did feel uncomfortable.

"Listen, I've got to go. There's a basketball game tonight."

Dave made a face like he couldn't think of anything less desirable.

"Oh, and what will you be doing tonight? Hanging out in some online forum talking about dragons?"

Suddenly, she felt bad. He actually looked hurt. She had only wanted to give back what he had been dishing out.

"Not everyone cares about basketball, you know? Or cheerleading for that matter," Dave said, looking mildly sad. Silver now regretted her previous comment, but was committed to being nonchalant. Not only had he made her uncomfortable, but now she felt guilty.

"Okay, whatever," she said brushing past Dave, not bothering to address him any further.

She continued down the hallway, the light from the door at the end growing brighter. Something bothered her about that interaction. He had been a dick to her and she had been a dick back, but she hadn't really wanted to hurt his feelings.

""Hey." It was Dave again. "Still looking for the English exam?"

She turned around and saw him standing in the same place she had left him. He had a huge smile on his face and a glint in his eyes that let her know she hadn't disabled him for too long.

Silver rolled her eyes and continued back down the hallway. She heard him laughing behind her.

This was going to be harder than she thought.

* * *

"Where have you been?" Anthony said, leaning on the passenger side of the car, sunglasses on.

"Talking to Dave," she said.

Anthony whipped his sunglasses off and his face lit up.

"You did?" he said.

"Don't get excited. We didn't have the talk."

His face fell and confusion replaced the excitement.

"So why were you talking to him?"

"He cornered me," she said, knowing this was only slightly true.

"You know, for someone you don't know or like, you sure talk to this kid a lot."

Silver didn't even want to respond. She just sighed and shook her head, reaching into her bag to look for her car keys.

"You seem kind of agitated," Anthony said.

"That's because I am agitated!" Silver exploded, happy to be able to take this out on her brother. She finally found her keys, slammed the car key into the door, and let herself and Anthony in.

He looked like he wanted to say something more and went to open his mouth.

"Anth, don't," she said in warning.

He closed his mouth and got into the car without another word.

They both buckled in, Silver turned the car on and then put on some music, hoping that Anthony wouldn't talk to her.

For a few minutes they sat in silence, listening to the music, Anthony looking out the window. Silver started to feel a little calmer as she drove the car, the motion putting her at ease. The trees on either side of the rode blanketed the car, making her feel protected from her own feelings, which were finally starting to fade.

"So, seriously, how are you going to bring this up with Dave?" Anthony asked, still looking out the window.

Silver felt jolted back to reality, and for a second wanted to reach over and hit her brother for reminding her of Dave. She leaned her head on her left hand, which was propped up on the side of the car door, keeping her right hand on top of the steering wheel.

"I don't know," she said, honestly. She had been so elated this afternoon at lunch, she hadn't really stopped to consider that now the really difficult task was ahead of her.

"Are you sure you want to do this?" Anthony asked her, looking directly at her now. She looked back over at him for a second.

"I'm so close," Silver said, eyes back on the road. "I've wanted this for so long. I'm almost there. And this one thing, one small thing is in my way."

"Silver, you'll do fine, even if you don't have the perfection you want."

She considered this, and even though he was being completely reasonable and trying to make her feel better, she felt herself growing angry once again.

"I don't want to be just fine. I want what I want," she paused briefly, then started again. "I've had this all mapped out, and this wasn't supposed to happen. I never thought I'd run into a problem with a grade, but I can't seem to make this happen. Grades were supposed to be the easy part, everything else was a little more difficult. But I made those things happen, and now the easy part is hard. I'm too far into this to just let it go now. Especially when there is a way to make it happen."

She could see him looking over at her, even though she didn't want to meet his eyes. She didn't want to admit to herself that she sensed pity in his gaze.

"You can always back out, you know. I'm sure Mike would also and at that point I'd be out of luck." She said this knowing that she was fully revealing her dependence on the two of them, and she didn't care.

"No, I'm still in. If that's what you want. I mean, I'll get something out of it, too."

She sat there, hearing what she knew he would tell her. She had known that from the beginning.

* * *

Silver walked into the gym to check the score of the JV game and to see how much time was left before Varsity was to play. Twenty-five years of sweat mixed with the scent of wood hit her nose in the familiar way that it always did.

This is what they all called the New Gym, even though it was edging its way toward three decades worth of use. The Old Gym was even darker, dirtier, and dingier and was only used for practices, which is where the cheerleaders were hanging out waiting for the game to begin. The boys' basketball team was still in the locker room, yet to emerge.

The cheerleaders had brought all of the banners, posters, and spears they had made the day before. Unfortunately, all of the left-over supplies had ended up in the trunk of Silver's car, so now every time she drove she heard the sound of a dozen cans of spray paint rolling around and knocking into each other. She would have to find a place to store them, but hadn't been able to think about it yet.

There was 2:38 left in the JV game. Their JV was losing—badly. Silver figured they were about ready to be put out of their misery.

The school that had come to play them was from across the state, a few hours away, and they were one of the best teams around. The boys' basketball team was as talented as it had ever been, and this year they were trying to play the best teams available.

Silver scanned the bleachers, taking in who was already here. They were starting to fill up. She saw some teachers from school and a lot of parents she recognized. The section where students usually sat was almost full.

"Hey, Silver. We're not late, are we?"

Silver turned around.

"Hey, guys," she said to a couple of senior girls that she was casually friends with. Jay had spoken to her, and her friend Marissa was by her side. "There's still a couple of minutes left for JV, but if you want a seat you'd better hurry. It's almost full."

"Okay, thanks," Jay said, as she moved quickly past Silver to find a seat. Marissa smiled at her warmly as she passed by, following Jay through the crowd.

Silver wasn't close with either of them, but ended up at enough social gatherings with the both of them to call them friends. They had become notorious after an incident in the beginning of the school year where they had gotten lost in the woods. After hearing the whole story, Silver couldn't believe some of the crazy situations people got themselves into. Fortunately, they had found their way out still in one piece.

Finally, the buzzer sounded to signal the end of the JV game, and Silver walked back out into the lobby that separated the two gyms on her way into the old gym.

"All right, guys, JV is over."

The other cheerleaders roused themselves from positions on the floor and the bleachers and began to gather up the banners and spears.

The team began to emerge from the locker room, looking a little too tightly wound. This would be one of their toughest opponents of the season and records, rankings, and bragging rights were at stake. Silver knew their nerves would settle down after a while, but right now they looked a little anxious.

"You guys ready to run out?" she asked Anthony as he came out from the locker room.

"Yup," he said.

"Good luck," she said, before turning back to the other cheerleaders to herd them into the gym and into position.

After each player had been given a spear, Silver got the cheerleaders into the gym and waited.

She saw the players line up outside of the doors ready to run in and begin warming up. Finally they burst through to loud cheers and applause.

The game had begun.

* * *

It was the third quarter and the game had been back and forth the entire time. Currently, the visiting team was up by three.

From the sidelines, Silver watched as Mike broke out ahead of the other players and Anthony passed him the ball. Mike caught it and deftly moved toward the basket to make an easy layup. The ball fell through the hoop and the crowd roared. To Silver, he always looked a little like he was floating when he shot a layup, gravity seeming to disappear for just a split second as his body went upwards toward the rim.

Between cheers, and in between glimpses of the game, Silver observed the crowd. The way that hundreds of people could suddenly move and yell as one being, no separation between any of them, was always fascinating to her.

She saw her mom and dad in their usual spot across from the bench, cheering Mike's last basket. Mike's mom and dad were a couple of rows in front of them. Without fail, no matter what was happening, Mike's dad looked irritated, and yelled out angrily at certain intervals. Silver's father could yell with the best of them, but no parent in the gym matched Mike's dad's intensity. Silver wondered what things were like in the house when Mike got home after a game.

She scanned the student section for friends and kids she knew, spying on a guy and girl who very clearly liked each other, but who weren't an established couple. Silver loved what she could find out looking into the crowd. She laughed a little at the secret she now shared with the two of them, but her laughter stopped as she moved her eyes to the left.

Sitting by himself with his feet propped up in an empty spot of the bleacher was Mr. Bailey.

He watched the game intently, as if he was studying something or reading a good book. He didn't cheer or make any kind of movement after they scored, just directed his eyes down the other end of the floor as the action moved toward the visiting team's basket.

Silver suddenly didn't feel that good. She felt her heart beating faster and her breath coming quicker.

She felt silly. She was sitting roughly fifty feet away from him. And he wasn't doing anything, just watching the game. Teachers came to basketball games all the time.

As she stared at him, every other body in the crowd went out of focus and Mr. Bailey became crystal clear. The outline of his body sharpened and the colors of his clothes and skin suddenly became very bright.

And then, he looked at her.

The expression on his face was the same as when he had been watching the game—intense, thoughtful, and focused. They were so far away from each other, Silver couldn't tell whether he could actually see her or not. But his gaze was like a laser beam. She swore she could almost see a path of light stretched out between the two of them.

Finally, he looked back at the game and watched as Anthony hit a short jumper. The crowd cheered.

He knows. Silver couldn't help thinking it even as she knew it couldn't be true. They had only just discussed this at lunch. Had one of them told someone? Had this somehow gotten around to Mr. Bailey?

No, that was crazy. Mike and Anthony had just as much reason as her to keep this a secret.

Silver was starting to feel warm, too warm. And her heart was beating ferociously. She tried to calm herself down, to tell herself that it was impossible for Mr. Bailey to know what they were planning. But his gaze. Maybe she was reading it wrong.

Her ears started to ring, and there were black spots appearing in the middle of the game. She glanced one more time at Mr. Bailey in the crowd, and just as she did he looked back at her. Then, darkness.

* * *

"Silver?"

She opened her eyes and found herself in the old gym, glad that it was darker and cooler in here. She must have passed out.

Rob was right in front her, and Nicole right next to him.

"Silver, are you okay?" Nicole asked.

"Yeah, I think. Did I pass out?"

"Yep, thank God you were sitting down. You just slumped right over onto me. Rob had to carry you out," Nicole said.

"It was really stuffy in there," Silver said as she rubbed her forehead with her hand, still lying down. Of course, she wouldn't mention the real reason she had gotten faint.

"Yeah, it was pretty warm in there. Apparently, Coach Bryan turns up the heat in the gym to try and throw off opponents," Rob said.

"Well, I don't know about that, but he certainly got you. Oh, here are your parents," Nicole said.

"Silver," her father said, as he came through the door to the old gym, his forehead wrinkled just as Anthony's would have, "are you okay?"

"Yeah," she said, as she started to sit up, "I got too warm in there."

"I'm not surprised," said a brusque feminine voice, "it was stifling." Her mother had walked into the old gym, and just as usual had a vaguely disapproving look on her face. Silver couldn't help but feel like she had done something wrong.

"Silvia, lay back down, don't get up yet," her mom said, while putting her hand on Silver's shoulder to press her back to the floor. Silver brushed her hand away.

Nicole and Rob had looked at her mom with puzzlement as they heard her use Silver's actual name. Nobody ever called her Silvia, except her mom, who never called her Silver.

A lot of people didn't know that Silver was just a nickname. Most people thought she had really free spirited parents who had given her an unusual name. Ha.

She was named after her mom's sister who had died before she was born, and who, despite the tragic circumstances of her death, her father had heartily disliked. He wasn't thrilled to have his only daughter share her name, and when the opportunity for a nickname came up, he jumped on it.

Apparently, when she was a little kid, she had so much energy that she was always running through the house. So fast, her father said, that as soon as she was in the room she was gone again, just like a flash of silver. She didn't know exactly what a "flash of silver" was, but to her father it seemed to make sense, and either way her nickname was born out of it. From that day on, her father had only called her Silver, and so did everyone else. Except her mother.

"Mom, I'm fine," Silver said, trying not to sound too annoyed. She sat all of the way up. "I just got too warm in there."

Her mother didn't say anything in response and her lips went back to the thin, tight line they usually kept.

"Sometimes that happens," her father said, in a tone of voice that told Silver he was trying to erase the tension. At this point, she just wished everyone would leave her alone.

"How's the game?" she asked.

"About the same as when you hit the floor," her dad said smiling, "it's only been a few minutes, you know."

"You should go home early," her mom said. Silver had been thinking the same thing, but now that her mom suggested it, she had suddenly developed a resistance to the idea.

"No, I'm going back to cheer," she said

"Silvia, you just passed out in a gym full of people, you need to go home," her mother said as if no other options existed.

"Mom, I can do what I want." The funny thing, though, is that what Silver wanted was to go home.

"We'll take you home. Leave your car here, Anthony will drive it home."

"Mom, I just got a little too warm. I'm not sick. I can drive and I can cheer."

"Silver," her father chimed in, "why don't you come home with us?"

Silver felt a little more apt to give in now that this was being posed as a question and not an order. She was ready to get out of here, and away from Mr. Bailey. She hated the thought of sitting in the car with both of her parents, but if she took the car, Anthony wouldn't be able to get home.

"Okay, I'll come home," she said, as she remembered that Rob and Nicole and been watching this whole exchange. She was a little embarrassed.

"What about the game?" Silver asked.

"It's almost over. Plus, it's not like it's the only game of the season," her father said in his usual carefree manner. This man could find the silver lining in a bomb going off in front of him.

Silver started to get on her feet, while both of her parents reached out to help. She was irritated.

"Guys, I'm not an invalid."

"We're just trying to help," her mother said and immediately Silver wanted to argue back, but thought better of it. If she didn't stop now, it would never end.

The five of them walked back out into the lobby and her father ducked into the gym to check the score.

"Bye, Silver. Hope you feel better," Nicole said, as she started to walk back into the gym.

"Yeah, Silver, feel better," Rob said as he followed her in.

"You know," her mother started, and Silver immediately tensed, "I never thought that one day almost no one would call you by your own name."

"That is my name," Silver said, her anger rising.

"No. That's some silly nickname your father gave you years ago. I prayed it wouldn't stick, but clearly God didn't hear me."

Silver looked at her mother with enough animosity to fill the entire lobby and both gyms. Her mother stood to her side, eyes directed toward the gym and not toward Silver. She stood a couple of inches shorter than Silver, which made her quite petite, as Silver was only average height herself. They didn't exactly look alike, but had the same coloring, and most people recognized immediately that this was her mother.

Her mother stood small, but erect, looking like she might snap if she made too sudden a movement. Silver, on the other hand, leaned back on her hip with one leg out in front of the other, almost as if she rested her weight on some invisible object propping her up, her arms crossed in front of her chest. She hoped her father would come out soon.

"Why don't you take it up with Dad then?"

"Believe me, I have," her mother said, still looking into the gym, not one muscle in her body moving.

Silver shifted her weight and vowed to remain silent. She wouldn't win this game.

Finally, her father emerged from the gym into the lobby.

"We're down nine, about six minutes to go," he said, his face a mixture of cheerful disappointment. His forehead wrinkled as he saw his wife and daughter.

"Ready to go?" he asked, slowing down as he moved toward them. Both Silver and her mother answered at the same time.

"Yes."

"Oh, wait a minute," Silver said, "I need my bag."

"We'll be out in the car," her father said smiling, putting one hand on her mother's back as they turned around to walk out of the lobby.

Silver walked back through the old gym, popped into the locker room, and grabbed her bag, heading back into the old gym as quickly as she had come through it.

She was thinking about having to ride all the way home with both of her parents, when she ran right into someone.

"Oh, sorry," she said, looking up to see who it was.

She had run right into Mr. Bailey.

"Silver," he said, his clear enunciation of her name jarring her, "your brother played a great game tonight. Unfortunately it looks as though their opponent will get the best of them." And then he added, "Too bad you had to miss part of it." He smiled, then continued on through the old gym and into the hallway that ran right outside of it, probably on the way to his classroom for something.

Silver couldn't help thinking it as she continued toward the lobby.

He knows.

CHAPTER 6

Silver lay on her made bed. She looked out the window, watching the clouds move in the sky. She had to focus to see the movement, but it was there. Those puffy, white marshmallows moved through the blue, changing shape slightly as they went along.

It was Saturday afternoon, the day after the boys' basketball game. Silver had been hanging around her bedroom today, door closed, not feeling the need to interact with anyone. She had straightened up, organized part of her closet and surfed around on the Internet, doing things, but nothing in particular.

She had been thinking about the night before. She replayed in her mind meeting eyes with Mr. Bailey and then her departure from consciousness. She felt his body hit hers when they ran into each other, and heard his crisp voice say her name.

The tension had started to build again, and she realized that she needed to get moving on recruiting Dave to her cause. The more her brain told her that this was impossible, the more her gut told her to get a move on.

She had no idea how to approach this. Granted, she seemed to run into Dave more and more these days. Really strange, considering she had never once spoken with him until a few days ago. And they disliked each other. Sort of.

Their interactions puzzled Silver. She didn't like Dave, but she wasn't convinced that it was dislike that she felt for him either. She just didn't feel comfortable in his presence. Not at all. The unease she felt when she spoke with him was unfamiliar to her. She didn't know how to categorize it. And it made her both dread and look forward to speaking with him again.

She was drawn to this situation in a way that she couldn't explain.

There was a knock at the door. A masculine knock, made with large, powerful hands. She thanked God it wasn't her mother.

"Yeah?" she asked.

"It's me." It was Anthony.

"Come in."

Her brother walked in wearing the team sweatpants and an old T-shirt that had a hole in the shoulder. He closed the door behind him.

"You've been hiding today," he said, sitting down on her bed and scooting his body over toward the wall, where he could lean against it.

"Maybe I have," Silver said, sitting up and positioning herself against the wall perpendicular to the one Anthony leaned on. Her legs were extended in front of her, but she had to bend them in order to avoid Anthony's outstretched legs, which were longer than the width of the bed. "I know you guys lost last night, but what was the score?"

"Eighty-two to seventy-seven," he said, making a face. "Peter ended up fouling out, which hurt us inside."

"Hmm," Silver said, then continued. "Mike did well, though."

"Yeah, he had twenty-eight points. But I'll tell you what, I'm glad I wasn't going home to his house last night. You should have seen his father's face after the game."

"He was angry at Mike?"

"Angry at him. Angry that we lost the game. Angry in general, I don't know. All I know is that he didn't look happy."

"Hmm," Silver said, not knowing what else to say. Poor Mike.

"So what happened last night?" Anthony asked, his eyes getting a little wider and his voice a little louder, looking like he hoped it would be a good story.

"What do you mean?"

"You passed out," he said, smiling like she should have known what he was talking about.

"Oh, right," Silver said, remembering the scene she had caused last night in the gym. "Yeah, I got too warm, and before I knew it my ears were ringing and everything was going black."

"Coach Bryan always turns up the heat before home games."

"That's what I heard," Silver said, looking down at her hands and picking at some peeling nail polish she had on. She wanted to tell him the real reason she had gotten faint, but hesitated. When she realized he was waiting for her to go on, she decided to tell him the story.

"Well, that's not the whole reason I passed out," she said, glancing up at her brother who leaned forward slightly waiting for her to go on.

"This is going to sound crazy," she paused, "Mr. Bailey was there. I saw him in the bleachers, and at one point he looked over at me, or I thought he did."

"Were you staring at him? Because you know how you can tell when someone's looking at you."

"Yeah, I know, maybe I was. But, he looked at me and it was like his eyes were laser beams that were going right through me. Like they could see into me," Anthony's forehead had wrinkled, "and, I don't know, I just started not to feel good." Silver looked up at her brother, who sat quietly, listening, his large body looking huge sitting on her twin bed. She didn't want to tell him the last part.

"I had this strange feeling," she started slowly, "that he knew."

"That he knows about what we discussed?"

"Yeah."

"That's impossible," Anthony said.

"You haven't told anyone?" This was the question she had been dying to ask him, even though she knew it was insulting.

"No, are you crazy?"

"Has Mike told anyone?"

"Definitely not."

They sat looking at each other for a moment, and Silver finally felt satisfied. Sort of.

"Silver, you don't have to do this if you don't want to. No one's pushing you. Mom and Dad would be fine with anywhere you wanted to go to school, so why not just let it go? Forget this whole thing with Mr. Bailey, get a B in English. Who cares?"

She considered for just a minute, gathering her thoughts, figuring out how to express what she felt. Anthony looked at her like he was looking at a creature he couldn't quite understand. One that fascinated him, but was too exotic for him to really feel comfortable with.

"Because it's my thing. Mine. Not anyone else's."

This answer had only fed his fascination and unease. Their eyes were locked with one another, and suddenly she felt she was pulling him toward her. Not his body, but something in his eyes. As he felt this pull, he wanted to look away, but couldn't. Finally, she broke eye contact and looked out the window at the clouds again. They had morphed into another shape since she saw them last.

"You know," Anthony spoke, "sometimes I think we're mostly alike, and then other times I can't figure out where you came from."

Silver chuckled, then gently kicked him in the leg.

* * *

It was Monday afternoon, and cheer practice had just ended. Silver needed a book from her locker, so she went back into the main part of the school to get it. She walked through the empty hallways with only the light from outside illuminating the way. Considering that it was December, there wasn't much light, but something about these dark, deserted corridors always made her feel peaceful.

She had been thinking about her task all day. About how to convince Dave to join them. She hadn't seen him all day. Partly she was relieved by this, and partly it made her anxious.

She needed to move fast; she didn't want this dragging on forever. She wanted to rip the Band-Aid off and get it over with. She knew the opportunity would present itself, she just hated waiting for it to happen.

She passed by the art room, and was surprised to hear noises and see a light on. Somebody burning the midnight oil, she thought on her way out of the side entrance.

She had never had much interest in artistic pursuits herself, and wondered about people who would stay for hours after school to work on a project.

Suddenly, she stopped dead in the hallway, and turned around back toward the art room. She peaked in.

There was Dave.

He sat at a canvas with brush in hand, making what looked like to Silver, very inconsequential brush strokes on his art. As far as she could tell, there was no one else in the room. He got up and walked into the ceramics room, which was off of the main room.

The school was old, and certainly not up to building code. She couldn't imagine that having a classroom that wasn't connected to a hallway was very safe, but then again, what did she know. A dark-room was also off of this main room, although that didn't seem as bad to Silver because there weren't thirty people sitting in that room on a regular basis.

She walked in and over to Dave's painting, and saw, once again, another dragon. This one was red, and more serpent like than the ceramic one in the art case. *What gives?* she thought, wondering if dragon art was all he did. She was still contemplating this when Dave walked back into the room.

"And once again, I find you admiring my dragon," Dave said, satisfaction in his voice and a can of paint in his hands.

"Do you make anything else?" Silver said, undeterred by his smugness.

Dave set the paint can down. He had on an old T-shirt, and—hopefully—an old pair of jeans, as they were both covered in paint. Silver thought she could even see some paint in his hair.

"Seriously, what do you want? This is the art room, not the gym."

"Thanks for letting me know. I get confused sometimes. Must be all the fumes from the leather and wood getting to me," she said, not feeling nearly as uncomfortable as the last time she ran into him. Her eyes returned to the painting automatically and she took in the image of the dragon once more.

"Okay, I have to ask," Silver said, unconcerned if this question would make her seem too interested, "what's with all the dragons?"

"I just like them," he said, shrugging his shoulders at the same time.

"So, do you do anything else?"

"What do you mean? Do I paint and sculpt other things? Of course."

"Well, where are they?"

"Do you want to see my whole portfolio? You've seen two pieces of my art. They both happened to be dragons."

"So what do you like about them?"

"I don't know. They're cool looking and fun to create."

Silver sat on the stool Dave had been sitting on. He made a face but didn't say anything about it. She noticed, but didn't care. She couldn't stop asking questions.

"Why is the background all orange and yellow? Is he in fire or something?"

"How do you know the dragon is a 'he'?"

She stared back at him, not understanding why he would ask her this question when she was asking him about the background. She must have looked perplexed because Dave just chuckled and moved on.

"I guess it could literally be fire, but I think maybe it's just supposed to evoke heat."

"Don't you know?" she asked him, trying to figure out why he wasn't sure when he was the one painting it.

He smiled again in the way someone does when a little kid does something cute they don't realize.

"Enough about dragons. What are you doing here?"

She was a little annoyed that he didn't answer her question. She actually wanted to know, and she realized that the small talk was now over.

"I just stopped in. Remember, I like to look at your dragons." She looked up challenging him to respond.

"You did not just stop in. If you expect me to believe that, you think I'm a giant idiot, and I'm insulted." He crossed his arms and leaned on the table, although he really didn't look angry, or insulted.

"You're right. I don't expect you to believe that."

Dave didn't move, but something washed over his face that Silver couldn't quite read. He remained leaning on the table top, arms crossed, face expressionless. She realized he was waiting for her to go on.

She debated the right way to start this conversation. What should she say as an introduction? Finally, she just decided to be blunt.

"I need a favor."

"Oh, do you?" Dave chuckled again, enjoying the fact that once again he had her at his mercy.

"Yes." Silver got up from the stool and began to pace around, glancing once more at the dragon. "You already know my biggest secret, but the even bigger secret is that I'm going to take your advice."

Dave now looked utterly perplexed as he tried to remember what advice he had given her.

"I still want the English exam and answer key, and I'm going to break in to Mr. Bailey's house to get it."

"That was a joke," Dave said, looking at her like she was the giant idiot, but looking a little scared, also.

"It might have been, but it gave me an idea."

Silver had made her way over to the windows and now stood looking out one of them at the parking lot outside. She suddenly felt perfectly calm.

"I'm going to his house to get the exam, but I'm not going to break in."

Dave's face changed to indicate that he knew where this was going. But he still didn't say anything. His eyes were locked directly onto hers.

"You have a key to his house." She didn't know this for sure, but figured if he fed Mr. Bailey's cats on a semi-regular basis, he probably just kept the key.

"And why would I give it to you?"

So he did have a key, she thought. Delighted that her prediction was correct, she continued.

"Well, you don't have to just give it to me. You can come along and let us in. And, of course, the exam key would be yours to use also."

"Number one, who is 'us'?"

She hadn't really wanted to mention Anthony or Mike until the end, but since the opportunity had arisen, she figured this was as good a time as any.

"My brother and his friend Mike."

"Why even have them come along at all? If I gave you the key, it would be easier to simply do it by yourself."

Damn. He was right. She hadn't thought about it like that. But, of course, when she planned this she didn't know if she could convince Dave to help, and she knew she needed someone. Now it looked like Dave might actually be amenable.

"Well, that's true, but I didn't know if you would actually help me."

"Which brings me to number two. I don't need that exam, so what's in it for me?"

This was exactly what she had expected him to say and was prepared. She was also becoming slightly impressed by the way he was playing this game.

Once again, she decided to be blunt.

"What do you want?" she said simply.

Despite his skill in negotiation, Dave suddenly looked like he had been caught off guard. He didn't move but began to eye her like he didn't quite know what to expect from her.

"Anything?" he finally asked.

"Anything," she said back.

Dave was expressionless again, and suddenly Silver began to worry. She had underestimated his ability in this situation, and now she was thinking she might pay for that mistake. She wished he would just hurry up and spit it out.

"Go to prom with me."

His words echoed throughout the room. Hollow, but enduring.

"Prom?" she squeaked out, sounding nothing like herself. She wished she didn't sound so afraid.

"Yeah, prom. Of all the things I could have asked for, I think that's fairly easy."

Dave now looked supremely satisfied with himself, the corners of his mouth turned up just slightly, his eyes challenging her.

She realized then that she had met her match.

This was worse than she thought. Prom was in public. And it was prom, which she didn't want to spend with dragon boy. But if this was what he was asking for, then it was her only way forward. She guessed it could have been worse. Maybe she could find some way out of it later, bargain with him for some other thing.

"Okay, deal." She tried to sound like she didn't really care that much, but she knew she wasn't doing a good job.

He started to walk toward her and for just a second she was scared. He stopped in front of her and put his hand out. He wanted to shake on it. She stuck her hand out and grabbed his, and his hand closed warm and firm around hers.

Suddenly she had the sensation that they were being pulled toward each other, not in body, but in some kind of energetic sense. For a moment her awareness of her body ceased, and she was simply her gaze, connected to Dave in a way that she didn't understand. The sensation of his hand on hers pulled her back again, and once more they were two separate bodies connected by just their hands.

She let go and so did he. He looked a little startled.

"So, uh," he got out, struggling to find words, "uh, what's next?"

"Um," Silver started, still gathering herself, "we need to plan this. All of us, the four of us. I'll let you know."

Silver suddenly felt like she needed to get out of there. They could work out the details later.

"All right, well," she said a little awkwardly, "I've got to go. I'll talk to you later."

"All right," he said, picking up a paint brush again and not making eye contact.

She started to walk out, then turned around.

"Thanks," she said, looking directly at him. He met her eyes again.

"No problem," he said.

As she was walking out, she noticed his jacket, which he had draped over a chair, and suddenly felt like herself again.

"By the way, you're not allowed to wear that during prom."

"Do you really think I'd wear that to prom?"

"I'm just letting you know."

"Thanks for the advice."

Silver walked back out of the art room and into the hallway. In a sense, that had been easier than she had anticipated, but in another sense, it had left her feeling unsatisfied.

She couldn't tell who had won.

* * *

Just a few minutes later, Dave put down his brush, and began to clean up the area he had been working in.

When his art was secured, and all the supplies cleaned and put away, he grabbed his jacket off of the back of the chair and started toward the door. He stopped for a moment, thinking he had heard a clinking sound. Realizing it must have been his keys, he patted his pocket to check that they were there, but felt only his leg through the denim.

He looked back at where he had been working and saw his keys on the table, remembering that he had taken them out of his pocket when he sat down to work.

He went back to grab his keys and finally left the art room, turning off the lights as he went.

After he had been gone a good thirty seconds or so, a hand reached out from the darkroom covered in bracelets and flipped the light back on. Her jewelry clinked together as she walked out into the art room with a couple of finished photographs.

Karly walked over to the near corner of the room where she had left her jacket and bag. Dave and Silver must not have noticed them.

As she walked out of the art room, flipping the light switch for the last time that night, she thought to herself that it might not be a bad idea if she could have a look at the exam questions too.

CHAPTER 7

The next day when school was over, Silver walked out to her car enjoying what was an unseasonably warm day for early December. There was no cheer practice that day so she was headed straight home.

This was nice because she had plenty of homework to do, and she told herself the extra couple of hours would come in handy. Although, in reality she knew she would probably just use that time to watch bad television and surf around on the Internet. Nobody would be home for a few hours, so she would have the house all to herself.

She stopped once she was outside to pull off her jacket, which in this weather was making her too warm. Silver draped it over her arm and adjusted her bag, continuing on to the parking lot.

She looked out from where she was at the fields that surrounded the school. The sun shone down on the grass and corn and trees, and for a moment she was struck by the simple beauty of it. Most of the time, she wished there was something around to get to at lunch or after school, seeing as how the school was literally in the middle of nowhere. But today she enjoyed the quiet and the natural surroundings, and didn't wish for anything more.

Many days, Silver got to school early enough to park in the upper parking lot close to the side entrance of the school, but today she had been later and so was in the far parking lot at the bottom of the big hill. Usually she minded the walk, but today she didn't.

She started down the hill, watching her footing as she went along as it was kind of steep. In the fall and spring, she would often see the field sport teams running the hill, and was usually glad she didn't play any field sports.

She finally reached her car and stuck the key in the lock to open the door. She threw her jacket and bag over to the passenger side and got into the driver's seat. But before she could close the door, she noticed a piece of paper on her windshield under the windshield wiper.

She got out again and grabbed the little piece of paper, knowing that it wasn't the right size for a ticket. And anyway, she had the correct permit and had parked in the correct lot. She unfolded it.

I want to talk to you. Meet me in the art room at 7 a.m. tomorrow.

That was an hour before school started, which meant she'd have to get here really early. The note wasn't signed but she could only imagine that it was from Dave if he wanted to meet in the art room.

As she stared at it, the handwriting struck her as odd. It was written in all caps, but had a feminine quality to it. She chalked it up to his being an artist.

She really didn't want to get to school that early, but if Dave wanted to tell her something, she had better meet him. She started to worry that he wanted to back out.

She chuckled a little bit at the thought of receiving this note. Not since elementary school had she written or received a note from somebody. Then again, Dave didn't have her phone number and she didn't have his, which was probably for the better.

Before she got back in the car, she resigned herself to getting here early the next morning. Then she crumpled up the paper and tossed it as far as she could from the car.

* * *

Silver opened the door to the school and stepped inside the quiet hallways. At five minutes to seven, she was the only car in the upper parking lot.

It had gotten cold again overnight, and she was already missing the unseasonable warmth of the day before. She had definitely needed her jacket this morning.

She told Anthony she had to get to school to meet with one of her clubs early and he hadn't questioned that. He did, however, grumble at having to get a ride this morning, since he also had to get a ride yesterday after practice. But Silver didn't care. Mike lived pretty close to them and always had a car to drive, so he could pick Anthony up, no problem.

She decided to go to her locker first to put down some of her stuff and she felt butterflies in her stomach as she walked to it.

She had started to feel somewhat comfortable with Dave, so she wasn't sure why she was feeling so nervous right now. Again, she was a little afraid he was backing out, but somewhere from inside of her she got the feeling that this wasn't what this meeting was about.

She peeked into Mr. Bailey's classroom as she walked by, and saw that he was already at his desk, typing furiously on his computer. She felt a pang of guilt at what she was planning to do, because, honestly, she didn't dislike him. Not that she felt particularly attached to him, either.

After putting her stuff in her locker, Silver began to make her way to the art room. *Déjà vu*, she thought as she reached the door and stuck her head inside looking for Dave. She didn't see anybody.

She stepped in and thought maybe he was in the ceramics room, so she walked over to the entrance and looked inside, but it was dark.

"If you're looking for Dave, he's not here."

Silver turned and jumped at the same time, looking like she might run out of the classroom. When she had settled down, she was surprised to see Karly standing in front of her.

"God, you scared me," Silver said, still too startled to feel angry. "Where were you hiding?"

"I was in the darkroom," Karly said, trying too hard to look poised. Silver noticed that her cheeks were flushed.

"Did you leave me that note?" Silver asked, cocking her head a little to the side, and realizing that this was not at all what she thought it was.

"Yep," Karly said, holding her ground, but looking a little nervous. Silver was confused but also interested.

"What did you want to talk about?"

"I want in."

Silver heard the words and immediately felt a shot of anxiety go from her stomach straight to her brain, leaving a hot, buzzing feeling in its wake. She wasn't going to give in so easily, however. She wanted to find out what Karly knew.

"You want in to what?"

Karly smiled a little and started to look just a little bit more comfortable. She looked Silver directly in the eyes.

"I want to come with you all to steal the exam questions."

At this, Silver's anxiety turned to dread as she realized that Karly knew exactly what she was talking about.

"What if I say no?" Silver was stone faced and stock still. She was not leaving this room without a fight.

"Then after you take the exam, I'll tell Mr. Bailey what happened. I'm sure you wouldn't want any attention drawn to the fact that you all suddenly got As on the final exam. Especially if Mr. Bailey already suspects that some cheating has occurred."

Silver was surprised at her response. She had expected her to say that she would go to Mr. Bailey or the principal right away, but waiting until after the exam was more clever, and, frankly, more detrimental to Silver. If Karly told someone beforehand, Silver could always deny it. To anyone else it would sound pretty ridiculous. But afterwards, that would be a problem. Silver decided to stall a little bit.

"How do you know about this? Did Dave tell you?"

"Dave didn't tell me anything. You guys just weren't very careful when you talked about this."

"But we were in this room. Alone."

"And I was in the darkroom. Alone. My stuff was piled on that stool, in the corner. I wasn't hiding. You guys just didn't notice I was here."

Silver felt stupid. She hadn't even thought to check the other rooms, assuming Dave was alone. This girl had her between a rock and a hard place, and, ultimately, she had no choice.

"Well, I guess you're in," Silver paused, accepting that she was trapped, and feeling bold once more. "I wouldn't think you would care too much about the exam grade."

"Why would you assume that? I want a good grade as much as anyone else." Karly actually looked offended, which Silver thought was a little ironic.

"Sorry, I just didn't think it was your thing."

Karly's face flushed once more, but not from anxiety this time.

"You're not the only person around here with ambition."

Silver was perplexed, and a little interested, by this. But she also wished that Karly would just stop talking.

"Listen, you've got me on my knees here. Just walk away with what you've earned. You got what you wanted."

Karly looked a little surprised to realize that she *had* gotten what she wanted. And for that, Silver knew she was a novice.

"So what's next?" Karly asked.

"We make a plan."

"Okay."

"Listen, I'll let you know. But we all need to meet."

"Okay. But remember, if you do this without me, I'm going straight to Mr. Bailey."

"I heard you the first time."

They both just stood there, not knowing what to say to each other. They were on the same team now, but they also couldn't ignore that Karly had just blackmailed Silver.

"All right, well, I guess I'll wait to hear from you," Karly said, picking up her bag and getting ready to leave the room.

"Okay," was all Silver felt like saying.

After another awkward pause, Karly simply turned around and walked out the door.

Silver looked at the clock on the wall: 7:04 a.m. That hadn't taken long, and she still had almost an hour to kill before class started.

She sat back on one of the tables, and rubbed her forehead with her right hand, wondering how this was already feeling out of control. She wished that she had just gone to Dave to begin with. He was right; it would have been so much easier. And now Karly was involved. Someone whose name she hadn't even known until a few days ago.

She had no choice but to keep moving forward.

Silver looked up then, putting her hand back down by her side, and found herself looking directly at Dave's dragon, which was propped up against the wall. It looked as if he had completed it.

She slid off the table, and walked out of the room, not sure where she was going to go next. As she did, she couldn't shake the thought that the dragon was watching her.

* * *

She hadn't been able to catch Anthony or Mike all day. And she certainly hadn't been able to get either of them alone.

She stood near the entrance to the boys' locker room, trying not to look like a stalker. She wanted to catch both of them before they started practice. This couldn't wait any longer.

She finally saw Mike walk out in a cut-off sleeveless T-shirt and shorts to his knees, his practice jersey in his hand.

"Mike!" she whispered loudly, then reconsidered the whispering. It only made her look guilty.

"Silver," he said, looking a little surprised.

"Where's Anthony?"

"He's still in there," Mike said, tilting his head back toward the locker room.

"When he gets out, I want to talk to you guys. Old gym."

Mike nodded and Silver walked away. Once inside the gym, she hoisted herself up on the short stack of bleachers that weren't pulled out, and leaned back against the wall.

The boys walked in a minute later and stood around her on the floor, leaning their arms on the bleacher she sat on.

"A small change of plans," she said. "So, Dave's in."

"Nice," Anthony said, "he can get us a key and everything?"

"Yeah," Silver said.

"That was easy," Mike said.

"It was pretty easy," Silver said.

"Why do I sense a 'but' coming," Mike said.

"But," Silver obliged Mike, "there's one more person coming too."

Anthony's forehead wrinkled. Mike chewed on his lip, eyes narrowed.

"Karly's coming with us," Silver said.

"Who's Karly?" Anthony said.

"You mean Karly with all the bracelets?" Mike said. "How did that happen?"

"Well," Silver said, trying to sound like she had this all under control, "she heard Dave and me talking about it and wanted to get in. I figured one more person could only give us an advantage in looking for the exam questions."

This was a lie, but it would be better if they thought she had this all under control. Even if she didn't.

"So wait, she was with you guys when you and Dave talked about this?" Mike asked.

"Well, not exactly. Dave and I were in the art room and she was in the darkroom next door and overheard us."

"So she was eavesdropping," Mike was looking at her suspiciously, "and then what, she came out and blackmailed you to let her come along?"

Both of the boys laughed at this.

Silver didn't laugh at all, and hoped that Mike would drop his questioning. She didn't really want to get into the details of how this happened.

"Look, the point is that Karly's coming with us and we all need to meet so we can plan this out."

"What about in the library sometime?" Anthony said, making the obvious suggestion.

"I don't know. Then everyone can see us," Mike said.

"Exactly, and if anyone asks, we're doing something for English," Silver said.

"When?" Anthony asked.

Silver considered. She wanted this to happen fast.

"Tomorrow morning, 7:30. If I can find Dave and Karly now. I think I know where they both might be."

Both boys nodded, neither one of them protesting.

"Assume tomorrow morning for now. If there's a change I'll let you guys know."

Silver hopped off the bleachers while Mike and Anthony headed back toward the new gym, their muscular arms swinging by their sides as they walked.

Silver headed straight out into the hallway from the gym. She knew exactly where she would check first. She just hoped they were alone.

As she walked into the art room, she saw Dave at his usual seat and looked around quickly for others.

"Are you alone?" she asked Dave, startling him as he turned around to see who it was.

"Not exactly, but we can probably talk in here."

"Is Karly in there?" she asked him, pointing at the darkroom.

"Yeah," Dave said slowly as if he wondered why Silver would know that.

"By the way, she's coming with us," Silver said as she walked into the darkroom. She had never been in here before. She heard Dave ask, "Karly?" before she was fully immersed in the room.

"I need you," Silver said, as she barged into the room, the odd light source confusing her and the smell of chemicals hitting her in the face.

Karly stood over a pan of liquid, swishing photo paper in it, while the picture slowly came to life. Silver was actually fascinated for a second before remembering what brought her in here. Karly jumped when she heard Silver's voice.

"You scared me."

"Well, I'm repaying the favor. We need to talk," and Silver motioned back toward the art room.

"All right, hold on."

Silver wondered why Karly was using a film camera for Photography and then assumed it must still be a part of the class. Their school was an old building and the darkroom wasn't going anywhere anytime soon.

Karly finished swishing around her photo, shook it off a little bit, and hung it up on a line like a piece of laundry before following Silver out of the room.

Dave sat quietly, still with a confused look on his face, waiting for the girls. Silver got to it right away.

"Tomorrow morning, 7:30. Oh, wait," Silver stopped and pointed into the ceramics room as if to ask if anyone else was here. Dave shook his head. "Okay. Yeah, so we'll meet tomorrow morning and plan this all out."

"That's kind of early," Karly said, to which Silver responded with the most incredulous look she could muster.

"Oh, right," Karly said, "that's fine with me."

"I could have just left a note on your car, but I figured I'd be a little more considerate." Silver couldn't help herself. Karly just rolled her eyes.

"Dave?" Silver asked.

"What did I miss?" he asked, looking back and forth between them.

"Nothing," they both said at the same time.

"Can you be here?" Silver pressed.

"Yeah, I can be here," Dave said.

"Okay. In the library," Silver said.

CHAPTER 8

It was 7:27 a.m. Silver and Anthony walked into the library and found a table, pulling over another chair so they would have five seats. Anthony sat down and yawned, not bothering to cover his mouth, and stretched his legs out underneath the table, hitting Silver's foot where she sat on the other side of the table.

"Sorry," he said, yawning again. She kicked him back.

"Pull a notebook out or something. Make it look like we're actually doing something," Silver said as she reached into her own bag to pull out some props. A textbook, a highlighter, some paper.

Anthony grabbed a book and pen and threw it onto the table. He looked at her as if to ask if she was satisfied.

"Good job," Silver said. She was getting tired of him already. He had been complaining all morning about having to get to school early. Not that he tried to back out or anything. But either way, she wished that he would just shut up.

Silver looked over as she heard the clink of metal on metal and saw Karly walk through the door. She looked a little nervous as she walked over toward the table where Silver and Anthony were, and Silver remembered that Anthony and Karly had probably never spoken before.

"Hey," Silver said as Karly sat at the seat they had pulled over, on a side perpendicular to where she and Anthony sat. "This is my brother, Anthony. Anthony, this is Karly."

Anthony raised a hand in a short wave, but didn't say anything. Karly waved and sort of half-smiled back, while saying hello to both of them.

Every single time she moved, her jewelry made massive amounts of noise, which was already irritating Silver. Karly fidgeted in her seat, and the noise made Silver think of the way the door opened and closed at a convenience store to alert the clerk that someone had entered. She made a note to herself to tell Karly to forget the jewelry when they went to Mr. Bailey's house.

"So where's everybody else?" Karly asked. Her voice came out soft and crackly.

"Um," she started, then spotted Mike, "well, there's Mike right now."

Karly seemed to brighten at having someone else here that she knew and was friendly with. Anthony perked up a bit too.

"Hey, guys," Mike said, sitting down in the seat next to Anthony, and flashing a big smile around the table. He turned specifically to Karly. "What's up?"

"Nothing," she said, her voice returning to normal as she said this. "I guess we're just waiting for Dave now."

"Silver, where's your new best friend?" Anthony asked.

"How would I know?" Silver responded, annoyed at the suggestion. She looked at her phone; 7:33 a.m.

"I don't think I've ever spoken to him once," Mike said. "Who is he friends with?"

"I think he's kind of a loner," Karly offered, "but he's all right though. People think he's really odd, but I think that's just because of that jacket he wears."

"So wait, do you have some art class with him?" Mike asked.

"No, I just know him because I'm usually in the darkroom when he's working on something after school. We just see each other around a lot."

"You take photography too? So, two of your four classes this semester are art related?"

"Yep," Karly said. "Next semester too."

Mike raised his eyebrows at this and nodded his head, then let
his gaze sink to the floor.

"There he is," Silver said as she watched Dave walk in wearing
his jean jacket.

Silver could see him look around the library then spot the table
they were all at. He made for it swiftly, but in the steady gait that he
usually kept.

He didn't look quite as nervous as Karly had, but Silver noticed
a little tension. He made eye contact with her first, and even smiled,
before he addressed the rest of the group.

"Hey," Dave said, pulling out the chair next to Silver. As he sat
down, his knee brushed by her thigh, and Silver was reminded of
the sensation she had in the art room when shaking his hand.

"Dave, this is my brother, Anthony. And this is Mike. Guys,
Dave."

Mike reached out across the table to shake hands, which left
Anthony no other choice but to do the same. Dave looked around
the table and noticed everyone's book and pens.

"I assume these are for decoy purposes," Dave said. Mike chuckled a little, but still eyed Dave like he was a specimen preserved in a
glass jar. Anthony eyed him also, with something like distrust, but
with a little fascination thrown in. Silver was surprised to hear him
speak next.

"Silver made us take all these things out so we wouldn't look
suspicious," Anthony said, giving her a little kick under the table
again, this time on purpose.

"Well in that case, I wouldn't want to piss off Silver," Dave said as he reached into his bag and pulled out a notebook. Afterwards, he pulled his jacket off and hung it on the back of the chair, revealing a plain black T-shirt.

"All right, so where do we begin?" Dave asked.

"Okay," Silver started slowly, actually at a loss for words, "well, first off, Dave, you have a key to his house, right?"

"Yep."

"Why do you have a key to his house?" Karly asked, and Silver remembered that she was a brand new addition to the group. This was just another thing she'd have to be filled in on.

"I feed his cats sometimes. Maybe three or four times in a year, so I just keep the key."

"So why even plan this then?" Anthony chimed in, looking pleased with himself. "You have a key. We find out when he's going to be out of the house, go over there, grab the exam, and we're out."

Silver looked at him a moment and realized how simply Anthony saw the world. She didn't know if she pitied or envied him.

"No," Silver said, "even though we're not technically breaking in, we're still entering his home without permission. We're not just going to wing it."

The word "trespassing" had come to mind, but Silver didn't feel like using it.

"Is he going to be out of town anytime soon that you know of?" Mike asked Dave.

Silver hadn't even thought to ask this. That would be the most ideal situation.

"No, I don't think so," Dave said.

"Why don't you just keep a look out for when he goes out and then give us all a call or whatever? You're neighbors, right? He's right there," Anthony said, which made Silver inwardly groan.

"Well, number one," Dave started, "we don't live on the same street. He's my neighbor, but he lives sort of behind me, and there are some trees separating us. I can walk to his house through my backyard and into his, but I can't really see his house from mine because of the trees."

"And, we wouldn't know how long he'd be out," Karly chimed in before Silver had the chance. That annoyed her. She felt like the new girl should be a little quieter, but she really had no room to enforce this.

Silver picked up her pen and tapped the end of it on the table, looking off to her right at nothing specific.

"We need to know specifically that he's going to be out and for about how long. We don't know exactly how long this is going to take us." She turned to Dave.

"Does he have any regular appointments that he keeps every week, or something like that?"

Dave leaned back and exhaled, his hand on his chin. This whole operation rested on him, and that made Silver nervous. For all practical purposes, she was the leader here, but at any time Dave could pull the plug. Finally he sat forward.

"He goes to the movies every Wednesday night."

"Every single week?" Mike asked.

"Yeah," Dave said, "he's big on routines, if you couldn't tell. We talked about this a while ago, but I'd bet anything he still does it."

"What time?" Silver asked.

"Eightish."

"Eightish makes me nervous," Silver said.

"Well, what do you want me to do," Dave said, "ask him directly what time he goes to the movies every Wednesday? It's a typical evening movie time. And remember I can always sneak over and check if he's still there. We don't need to know the exact time. You figure he'll be gone two hours, at least; if we're off by a little that's okay."

"What about your parents?" Karly asked. "Won't they be suspicious when four new friends come over and we're all sneaking around your neighborhood."

"My mom will be at work, and my dad doesn't live with us."

This was new information to Silver, and she filed it away in her mental storage cabinet.

"That reminds me," Silver said, directing her thoughts to Anthony, "what about Mom and Dad? I mean, I guess we could always make up something, but on a school night it would have to be pretty good. I don't know how late we'll be."

"Mom and Dad are going away next week, remember?"

Silver felt a thousand light bulbs go off in her body as her energy soared. She couldn't have hoped for better.

"I didn't know that," she said.

"They told us the other day. I thought you were there. Oh well, whatever, they're going to be away. Mom has a business trip to somewhere cool, so Dad's going with her."

"That's perfect then, we could do this next Wednesday. Mike, what about your Mom and Dad?" Silver said.

"I'll just tell them I'm over at your house. That's easy enough," Mike hesitated here, "but how late do you think we'll be? They'll probably want me back on the early side. If we go past that ..." Mike stopped here, but Silver knew what the rest of the sentence contained.

She suddenly felt nervous about Mike's involvement. He was loyal and trustworthy, but his father was also more vigilant than any other of their parents. She wasn't sure about Karly, but she couldn't imagine either one of her parents topped Mike's dad.

Mike was working with more stringent rules, that wouldn't go unnoticed if broken. Dave sounded like he was pretty much on his own. At least for next week, she and Anthony were on their own. But Mike had people watching him all the time.

"Mike," Silver tried to sound gentle, "you don't have to actually come with us." Silver stopped here to gauge his facial expression and then had an idea. "Karly, you don't actually have to come either. The three of us can go over and we'll share anything we find. It might actually be easier—" Silver never got to finish.

"No," Karly said, looking directly at her. "I want to go with you guys."

Silver expected this answer, but hoped she would hear something different. She didn't know if it was a lack of trust or simply the sadistic purpose of keeping Silver under her thumb that made Karly want to go, but whatever it was, Silver once again wished it wasn't there. She had been so stupid not to check to see that she and Dave were alone that day.

"Okay," Silver backed off Karly, but she still had a chance with Mike.

"Mike?"

He looked down at the table, his hands clasped in front of him on the tabletop looking like he was fighting an internal battle.

"If your Dad's going to be a problem, you can always—" Once again, Silver was cut off.

"No," Mike said, looking directly at her, "I'm coming."

She realized that mentioning his dad at that moment had probably not been the right approach.

"If we go over to his house around eight, we should be finished in plenty of time for me to get home," Mike said.

In her mind, Silver added the word *hopefully* on to Mike's sentence before she could stop herself.

This group was becoming top-heavy, and at any moment Silver felt it could fall over before they had the chance to pull this off. Or even worse, while they were trying to pull this off. She wished once more that she had simply gone to Dave first. Then she'd feel comfortable.

"Now when we get to his house, what are we actually looking for?" Karly said, and once again Silver was annoyed at her participation.

"What I think is—" Dave started.

"What you *think*?" Mike asked, leaning a little forward. "'Cause we can't go on what you think."

Oh yes we can, because it's the only thing we've got, Silver thought, glad that she had control enough of her mouth not to say that out loud.

"Look, you have to understand how," Dave paused and looked up as he searched for the right word, "orderly he is." He then looked over at Mike. "But, here's what I *know*. A couple weeks or so before he gives the exam, he'll prepare the questions and print them up. He'll have them in a folder."

Dave stopped here and looked around, and Silver found her curiosity growing.

"What he'll also have in that folder is an answer key."

"Nice," Anthony said, saying what they all felt.

Silver felt the lights go off in her body again, excited to realize there was an answer key also. She had only been hoping for the questions.

"How do you have an answer key to an essay exam?" Mike asked, looking suspicious.

"There will be three or four bullet points of things that he's looking for in the essay underneath each question. This will be stapled to the inside, left-hand side of the folder."

"Why?" Mike asked.

"Look, I'm just telling you what I saw," Dave said.

"You've actually seen all this?" Silver asked.

"Yeah, this is two or three years ago. Wasn't very useful to me at the time. One of the bedrooms is an office, there was a folder on the desk in there. I was just looking around."

"For as careful as he is, you wouldn't think he'd leave that lying around," Anthony said, and Silver was pleased he had actually said something intelligent.

"Why wouldn't he? It's in his home. At the time, those questions were of no use to me, and besides, he trusts me. I mean, he lets me keep a key to his house."

"So next Wednesday, we're a week out from the exam, so you think he'll have them prepared?" Silver asked.

"I know he will," Dave said.

"You know, you'd think if he was so worried about people cheating, he'd just pick the questions he wanted and write them up on the board or something. Paper just seems so ancient," Anthony said and Silver gave him another tick mark in the intelligent column in her mind.

"Old habits die hard after thirty-seven years," Dave said, shrugging his shoulders.

The rest of the table nodded their heads and looked around at one another.

"Do you know where that folder will be? I mean, I guess we can bet in the office, but where exactly?" Silver asked.

"Well, I'm not sure. He's got a ton of file cabinets, and a desk with several drawers, so I would imagine it's somewhere in one of those. We'll have to look a bit, but I bet it's well labeled."

Silver thought back to all of the papers she found from the eighties in his classroom and hoped he had pruned his home files a little better. Probably not, she figured.

"Okay," Silver began to recap, "we have a key, we know he's out on Wednesday evenings, we know what we're looking for and where it will be for the most part. What are we missing? Anything?"

The five sat for a minute thinking, trying to figure out what else they needed to talk about.

"Hey, there, folks."

This time, all of the lights in Silver's body exploded.

Mr. Bailey walked by, strolling through the library presumably to get to his classroom. His blazer was well coordinated with the sweater he wore over a crisply ironed shirt, the collar of which was visible. His tall, straight frame wore all of his clothes well, and, though always purposeful, never looked hurried.

"You all look hard at work," he said with an approving look, not slowing his pace, "see you in a few minutes."

He exited the library on the other side of the room as smoothly as he had entered.

Everyone at the table looked stunned. Nobody had been able to say a word to him. Silver looked around at everyone and saw her shock mirrored back to her. Finally, Anthony started laughing.

This caused the rest of the table to lapse into giggles, dissolving the tension.

"What are the chances?" Anthony asked, leaning forward over the table.

No one else had anything to say.

Unfortunately, they had caught the ear of the librarian, who gave them a dirty look, but didn't seem to want to move from her chair to speak to them. They settled down, each one individually deciding they probably shouldn't draw any more attention to themselves.

Silver looked at her phone again. They only had a few minutes.

"Okay. So next Wednesday, how are we going to meet up? Dave, do you want to check on his house around eight and then let us know if he's gone?"

"Yeah, that's probably a good idea. I'll give you guys a text when I know for sure."

"No," Silver said, "no texts. Call me and call Karly. I'll let these two know," she indicated Mike and Anthony, "and we'll all come over."

"Why don't I just come over to your house earlier, so the three of us will all be there?" Mike said. "Also, then there won't be a ton of cars at Dave's house. Karly, where do you live? Do you want to come by too?"

Silver inwardly groaned at Mike's suggestion. Karly told them where she lived, and luckily, it wasn't close to Silver and Anthony's house.

"It's probably just easier for me to drive myself, honestly," Karly said.

They all sat there for a moment realizing that they were probably about done.

"So it's all settled?" Dave asked, starting to grab his jacket from the back of his chair.

"Yeah, it's all settled," Silver said, and then had another thought. "By the way, no texts or e-mails about any of this. In-person communication would be best, but the phone is okay too."

They all nodded their heads and began to gather up their things.

"Oh, and no idiotic postings about this, or any hints of it, anywhere online," she added, unfortunately having to add this in. When it came to the Internet, people just couldn't help themselves.

"We're not complete idiots," Karly said, giving her a look.

"I felt the need to state that directly," Silver said. "Oh, and no jewelry that night either. We don't want to announce ourselves to the whole neighborhood."

Karly didn't say anything back, but looked as if Silver had just commanded she show up naked.

"All right, then, see you guys in class," Dave said as he stood up from the table. Silver watched him walk out and felt like she wanted something more from him. His exit bothered her. Although, really, he had given her everything she wanted. And he had been perfectly cooperative, which surprised her a little. Granted, he was getting something out of the deal also. At the thought of their agreement, her stomach turned a little bit. She hadn't told anyone why Dave had agreed to help them. She thought about showing up somewhere in public with him and didn't know how she would explain it.

Anthony and Mike got up, said good-bye to the girls, and headed out the door together, laughing about something, the details of next Wednesday evening out of their thoughts already. She did admire her brother's ability to—she didn't quite know how to explain it—push things out of his mind when they weren't necessary.

It was just her and Karly left.

"Satisfied?" Silver asked, her anger finally getting the best of her.

"Do they know why I'm here?" Karly asked, knowing full well that Silver hadn't told anybody about what happened.

"No," Silver answered simply, having nothing else to say.

Karly made a sound like a laugh, but there was no humor in it. She packed up her stuff and got up from the table.

"Bye, Silver."

The sound of her voice reverberated to Silver in a way that was profoundly unpleasant. And for some reason, it bothered her that she had said her name. The way that she had held it on her tongue.

Silver said nothing in return, and watched her walk out the same way that she had watched Dave walk out. But instead of wanting to call her back, she felt the urge to get up and push her out the door. To send her presence as far away from her as possible.

After a minute or two of fiddling around with her pen and textbook, she gathered up her stuff and left the library.

She hurried a little through the hallways, trying to make it on time to class, and not wanting to run into any of the people she had just spent the last half hour with. She didn't feel as good as she thought she should, what with everything coming together just as she wanted.

The bell rang as she crossed the threshold of the classroom. She was the last one to sit down.

"Silver, you've slipped in just in time," Mr. Bailey said as he grabbed a pen off his desk to mark the attendance.

She smiled at Mr. Bailey and out of the corner of her eye saw Dave glance back at her as she sat down in her chair.

CHAPTER 9

Silver walked through the doors of the church, and couldn't remember why she was here. She looked down at herself and realized that she was wearing the dress she had worn for her confirmation. Two years prior.

She turned around and watched Anthony walk through the door in a dark suit. He smiled at her strangely, and as she looked at him the outline of his body seemed blurry, like she couldn't focus on him. He simply stood, smiling.

She went to ask him why they were here. Why they were getting confirmed again when they had already done it, but no sounds came out when she moved her mouth. She tried again and again, but still no voice. Anthony smiled.

They walked up the aisle, and Silver was surprised to see that a line had formed in front of the altar. It seemed that they had arrived here mid-ceremony. They were the last.

The line was really long. From where she stood it seemed like a mile up to the bishop who, she knew, anointed each individual as they stood before him.

But, it was strange. Each one stood alone and not with the sponsor that was supposed to accompany them. Silver wondered where her sponsor was, her uncle, it had been. Her father's brother.

Her father. Where were her parents? There was no one else in the church except the bishop and the long line of young people awaiting their confirmation.

She looked at the stained glass on the walls and saw the colors dim. The pictures dulled without the sunlight behind them. It was night.

Fear crept up on her as she realized that this wasn't how this was supposed to go. She turned around to look at Anthony behind her, but he was gone. She turned around and silently waited for her turn.

Silver couldn't feel or see her legs moving, but she was getting closer and closer to the bishop. She could now see the front pews filling with those individuals who had already received the sacrament.

She looked to her left, and to her surprise saw Karly sitting quietly. Karly looked at her then got up and walked down the aisle behind Silver, toward the doors. Her jewelry clinked together in a deafening sound, reverberating throughout the church.

Silver was afraid of disturbing the ceremony, and turned around to tell Karly to take her jewelry off, but when she looked behind her Karly was gone, although the sound echoed through the church.

Silver felt she should apologize to everyone, but when she looked, no one seemed to have noticed. She felt relieved.

She was now five people from the front, and though she knew that there was nothing to be afraid of, her fear had reached a crescendo. Finally, it was her turn.

She stood in front of the bishop, who held a bowl in his hands. She thought she was supposed to say something, but couldn't remember what it was.

As he brought his hand to her forehead, her fear dissipated, and she realized that this was almost over. She had never had anything to worry about. He touched her with the oil.

Just as she was about to sit down with the others, she noticed the bishop looking at her strangely. She suddenly felt exposed. She turned around quickly to face the others and saw what the bishop must have seen on her.

The oil on their foreheads had turned to blood. It dripped down their noses and onto their clothes. Some people had brought their hands up to stop the flow, and it now covered those too. She saw Anthony again, his hands red and slick.

"Silver, I have blood on my hands," he said, and then Silver turned back around.

The bishop was looking into his bowl at the dark red liquid inside and then looked up at Silver as if to ask what she had done. He dropped it, horrified, and the bowl shattered on the altar, the blood spilling over the ceramic shards.

* * *

Silver woke with a start, her heart racing and sweat on her forehead. She brought her hand up to it and checked her fingers. It was Wednesday morning.

CHAPTER 10

Silver was anxious. She didn't want to admit to how much.

The morning went by in a fog, with her and Anthony not saying much to each other except for when they knocked into each other trying to use the bathroom sink at the same time.

Normally, with their parents away, the house would become much more peaceful, each of them feeling freer than they normally would. The TV was double the volume it was usually at, they played whatever music they wanted throughout the house, dishes would pile up in the sink, and, in general, they simply did whatever they wanted, not having to clash with the adults that were normally there.

But this time after their parents had left, the house remained strangely tense. And both of them had mostly kept to themselves.

At school, Silver loosened up a little with all the distractions that normally presented themselves.

Even sitting in Mr. Bailey's class was okay, although she couldn't make eye contact with him or even look in his direction. She busied herself with what was presented and tried not to think too much about that evening's plans.

She didn't speak to Mike or Karly or Dave, not feeling in the mood. Dave kept turning around, she assumed to catch her eye and say something, but she wouldn't look at him. She did, however, notice that whatever book he was reading had a dragon on the cover. He had laid it on the floor next to his bag like he always did. She wished she hadn't seen it.

The rest of the day went by. Too quickly or not quick enough, Silver couldn't decide, but either way it finally ended.

Mike caught up with her and Anthony as they were walking to the car, and let them know he'd be over in a couple of hours. They had plenty of time before Dave was to call them so that was fine with them.

They drove home in silence.

Silver kept running through the plans in her mind, looking for something she had missed, ruminating over the details. It was really very simple, which, for some reason, made her more nervous than she thought it should.

At home, she couldn't concentrate on anything. And watching TV or surfing the Internet just made her feel restless. She changed her clothes and went down to the basement where there was a treadmill. She put her earbuds in and ran, the sweat and the heat and the exertion making her feel better. She ran until she couldn't stand it anymore.

Then she showered and dressed again, feeling slightly better than she had before. The waiting was killing her.

Mike came over and played video games with Anthony as if this were any normal night of the week. None of them mentioned Mr. Bailey, or Dave, or the exam.

Then, Silver's phone rang.

"Hey. He's gone. You guys can come on over."

She had never spoken to Dave on the phone before, and hearing his voice without seeing him in front of her was strange and interesting. His voice was pleasing to her in a way that she had never noticed before, and she wished that he would keep speaking to prolong the pleasant reverberation his voice had in her ears.

"Okay, we'll be right over. So like ten minutes probably. Have you called Karly?"

"No, I called you first. I'm just about to."

Silver had the strange sensation that she had won some kind of competition, and was pleased with herself.

"Okay, see you in a few minutes." She hung up the phone, and didn't immediately call out to the boys, who were still playing video games, but stood for a moment, feeling strange but more at ease than she had been all afternoon.

"That was Dave. Let's go."

Mike and Anthony stopped their game and got ready to go.

"Hey, aren't we supposed to be wearing masks or something?" Mike asked, smiling just a little too widely.

Anthony laughed as he remembered his previous idea, and the two boys began going back and forth regarding the proper wardrobe for breaking into someone's house. Silver wished they would both shut up and get in the car. Their laughing was making her nervous again.

"I'll drive," Silver said, and tried to think about anything she might need. Dave had the key. That was the only thing they needed. Still, she felt unprepared leaving the house.

Silver, Anthony, and Mike got into the car, with Anthony in the passenger seat and Mike in the back. The two of them were still having a completely inane conversation that was driving Silver to the brink. She guessed it was probably better than silence, but their voices grated on her in a way that was almost unbearable.

Their conversation kept up all the way to Dave's house and after a few minutes, Silver was actually glad that she didn't have to speak. She saw the five of them opening the door to Mr. Bailey's house and going through his office over and over again in her mind. But when she tried to imagine them leaving the house, the door would suddenly stick or someone would knock over a shelf or something would happen that wouldn't allow them to leave. She willed her imagination to let them leave the house, but it would not obey her.

Finally, she pulled onto Dave's street and starting looking for his house.

"Would you guys help me look, please?" she said, her irritation toward them bubbling over.

"What's the number again?" Mike asked, sounding like he genuinely wanted to be helpful.

"Seven oh three," she said.

Dave's street was dark. No sidewalks. No streetlamps. The only lights were from the houses themselves, porch lights and glowing windows.

The homes on the street were detached, but small. One-story ramblers that had probably been built fifty years ago. Silver's neighborhood was much newer, with more modern accoutrements, and to her, these homes looked plain and unaccessorized, though, probably, peaceful and cozy.

She could make out the line of trees behind the homes on the left side of the street, Dave's side, according to the odd numbers she saw, and realized that Mr. Bailey's house was somewhere beyond those. They were very close now.

"That one's 701," Mike pointed out a house where the porch light shone brightly on the house numbers making them very easy to see. That was good, because the next one, which they knew must be Dave's, wasn't as bright. The only light was what peaked out from behind the curtained windows.

Silver pulled into the driveway with a carport that had one car parked under it; an older compact car with a few stickers on the back of it. She guessed that was Dave's car.

She thought for a moment that maybe she should have parked on the street so as not to block him in, but then remembered that they would be walking. Karly could park on the street.

She turned the car off and nobody moved for a moment.

"This is it," she said, and everyone pulled their door handle at once.

She felt weird walking up to Dave's door, like they were all there to hang out or something. That would never happen.

As she walked up to his front step, she could finally see his house number, though the 3 was hanging upside down by only one nail. Clearly, neither Dave nor his mother was very worried about the condition of the house. A part of her wanted to search for a nail in his house, and fix it before they went over. It was such a small repair she wondered why they hadn't done it. Finally, she knocked.

The door opened after just a few seconds, and there stood Dave in a T-shirt and jeans. Silver smiled.

"Hey guys," Dave said, not really smiling, but not unwelcoming either.

The three of them stepped into his home, awkwardly standing around near the front door, not sure what to do or say.

"Did you get a hold of Karly?" Mike asked, breaking the silence.

"Yeah, she said she'd be right over."

Silver glanced at her phone. She figured they would be here before Karly, but she hoped she would hurry up.

"You guys can sit down, turn on the TV if you want," Dave gestured to the living room. The boys went and sat down, somewhat timidly.

"Actually, do you mind if I use your bathroom?" Silver asked.

"No, it's the last door on the right," Dave pointed down the hallway that Silver assumed led to the bedrooms.

"Thanks," she said as she started down the hallway, having to get around a few boxes that were lined up against the wall. It was dark, and she looked around for a light switch, but couldn't find one so she just continued making her way to the last door on the right.

When she got to the bathroom, she reached her hand in along the wall and found the light switch, which illuminated the hallway a bit also.

There were three other doors and she found herself curious about which one was Dave's bedroom.

As she left the bathroom, she heard the sound of the TV in the living room and didn't hear any new voices, which meant Karly wasn't there yet. She decided to take a look around.

She peaked into the bedroom at the very end of the hall, which must have been Dave's mother's room. She didn't walk in as she didn't want to intrude on her privacy.

She turned back down the hallway, and stuck her head in the next room she came to, the one that was located adjacent to the bathroom. This was definitely a young male's bedroom. She looked over her shoulder back toward the living room, and walked inside, flicking on the light. The room was covered in artwork.

Ceramic sculptures and canvases covered the walls, the floor, and all available surfaces. A pair of jeans and a couple of T-shirts littered the floor and the bed. She looked around for some photos, or any other personal effects beside the artwork, but didn't see any. She wondered why.

Apparently, Dave did create more than just dragons, although dragons made up at least half of the work. They were all different sizes, colors, and shapes. Some looked like the type of dragon the hero has to slay before moving on with his journey. The type that lies in front of his treasure all day, breathing fire when he gets bored. Some others looked more like snakes.

There was one that Dave had painted that was completely white and sinewy, with blue eyes. The eyes drew Silver in, so that she couldn't focus on the rest of the dragon's body. When she tried to look away, she couldn't, and it seemed to follow her around the room.

There was a small bookshelf that rose halfway up the wall. It was crammed with books. She picked a few up, but didn't recognize any of them. Not that she ever really read, but just in case.

She had the urge to touch all of his belongings. To walk through this maze of intimate items and take a part of him when she left here. There was nothing too ordinary for her in this room.

His closet was partly open, and a couple pairs of shoes had spilled out. The bed was unmade, though the navy colored comforter had been pulled up over the bed so you at least couldn't see the sheets. It wasn't exactly messy, just neglected. The walls were an off-white as if they had never been painted since the house was built. Nothing except the artwork covered the walls.

It struck her that there was something strangely blank about this room, with the exception of the art and the books.

That thought made her feel a little sad, and compassion sprung up from within her. Though for what, she didn't know.

She flicked the light back off, but could still see the white dragon pretty clearly. As if it had absorbed the light, and now reflected it back to her in the dark. She turned around and left the room, feeling strangely unsatisfied.

Silver walked back to the living room and was surprised to see the three boys actually talking to each other. She glanced into the kitchen at the microwave to check the time. Karly should have been here by now.

She sat down on the floor in the living room and leaned up against a wall. Dave was in a chair and Anthony and Mike were on opposite ends of the couch. She didn't feel like getting in the middle.

She drifted off into thought, leaving the TV and the conversation behind. She felt better than she had at her house. She wished Karly would get here though. Then this could be over with.

"I think that's her," Dave said, bringing Silver back to the living room. Silver turned to look out the window and saw headlights through the gap in the curtains. The car they belonged to was parking on the other side of the street.

A minute later there was a knock on the door, and Dave got up to open it. Karly stepped in, sans most of her jewelry. She still wore a few bracelets and a large green ring, which irritated Silver, as she was sure the bracelets still probably made noise. But, really, it didn't matter. They would be in his house alone. She decided she should be glad Karly hadn't worn her full regalia.

Karly stood close to the door, not fully entering the house, while Anthony and Mike stood up from their spots on the couch.

"Looks like we're ready," Dave said, and Silver both admired and resented his leadership. This was her mission to run.

Dave grabbed a key off the key hook that hung on a piece of leather string. He put the key around his neck and guided all of them toward the back door.

It was dark outside, really dark. And cold.

It took a moment for Silver's eyes to adjust, but when they did she could just make out the trees that separated Dave's house from Mr. Bailey's house.

"Wow, it's dark out here. Maybe we should grab a flashlight or something," Anthony said.

"No," Dave said, "I know my way."

They all followed Dave as he began walking toward the edge of his yard, leading them into the trees. The leaves crunched as one by one they entered this small tract of forest.

Silver tried to step gingerly as she walked, afraid of stepping on something that might attack her, or maybe even pull her into the undergrowth, where she imagined she would be trapped forever in the dark, in the cold. She hated putting her feet where she couldn't see, but even as her fear grew she could see the edge of the trees, and Mr. Bailey's yard on the other side.

She thought about snakes hiding in the leaves, resting, their bodies curled up into a coil. She thought about the serpent-like dragons in Dave's bedroom, and imagined those curled up beneath the leaves. She couldn't tell if this was more scary or less.

Finally, they were back in the grass, their feet traipsing over short, winter grass. Only now they were on the other side. They were in Mr. Bailey's yard.

His house looked similar to Dave's and Silver was sure it was a similar layout. It was completely dark. No lights peeked out from cracks in the curtains. This surprised her. Her parents always left a light on when they all went out.

No one spoke. Dave walked to the back door and opened it swiftly; Silver could barely see him put the key in the lock. There was no dead bolt on this door, just the one knob.

The four of them followed Dave inside, and Silver, the last one in, shut the door behind them. It was silent.

The first thing Silver saw in the darkness was two glowing circles, seemingly suspended in mid-air. *The dragon.* No, a cat, she realized. Mr. Bailey had cats.

She watched as Dave walked over to the cat in its position on top of the couch, and patted it on the head. As the cat tilted its head toward Dave's hand, the eyes disappeared.

Something brushed by Silver's leg, startling her, when she realized that it was another cat. Her family didn't have pets and she wasn't used to sharing a house with animals.

The cat continued to rub against Silver, making it hard for her to walk forward. She was shocked. Frankly, she didn't like cats that much.

"Does this mean the cat likes me?" Silver asked, looking down at her feet, puzzled.

"Shockingly, yes," Dave said, and Silver heard him laugh.

"How many cats does he have?" she asked.

"Three. Golden," Dave pointed at the cat still wrapping itself around Silver's legs, "Stripes," he indicated the cat on the couch, "and Atticus is around here somewhere."

Silver bent down to the cat that wouldn't leave her alone, and reluctantly put her hand on its head, feeling the little scull beneath the short fur. She didn't know what the cat wanted, but she ran her hand down the length of its body also, where she could feel the ridges of its spine. She felt the cat vibrate in return, and knew enough to know that a purr meant the cat was enjoying itself.

"Looks like you made a friend," Dave said.

Silver didn't say anything back. The more the cat liked her, the guiltier she felt. She stood up.

"Okay, let's get to it."

"His office is over here." Dave motioned toward one of the bedroom doors.

Anthony stepped in first, being the closest to the door, and flicked the light switch.

"No!" Silver yelled, annoyed that she hadn't been the one to walk in first.

Anthony turned around, looking shocked that Silver was upset, and flicked the light back off.

"The neighbors might see!" Silver said.

"Won't they just think it's Mr. Bailey?"

"I have no idea what they might think, but we definitely don't want them to think that the house has been broken into."

"Okay, but how will we see?" Anthony asked.

She pushed her way past the others into the office and pulled up the blinds on the lone, small window in the room. It gave them a little bit more visibility. Silver tried to remember if she had seen the moon tonight, but didn't think she had. Maybe it was just behind cloud cover. But maybe it was a new moon.

"Okay, this is what we have to work with," she said to the group, who didn't look very happy at the conditions they had to search under.

"Dave?" Silver said, giving him the floor in case he had any more instructions.

"Start searching," he said with a shrug of his shoulders.

They all piled into the room, and picked a spot to start looking. It was crowded with the five of them in there. Something else Silver hadn't thought about.

Silver started in the most obvious place first. The top of his desk.

There was one manila folder on it and she thought they might have gotten lucky. She opened it to reveal a stack of student authored papers, not from her class judging by the names of the first few papers. Her excitement deflated.

That was all for the top of the desk. No other papers, no other folders, just a closed laptop and a desk calendar with today's date on it. Not an errant pen or piece of paper or any personal effects. At least he had made it easy on her. She tried the drawers next.

Silver opened them one by one to reveal lots of small items, but no papers. Both of the bottom drawers were empty. She turned around to find a file cabinet that had not yet been searched.

Déjà vu, she thought to herself as she opened the top drawer of a file cabinet across the room from the desk. There were seven cabinets total, so there would be two more to search after they were done with these. She was surprised that he had seven file cabinets in a room this size. But then she thought to herself that she was surprised after all those years of teaching he only had seven. The room was silent as everybody concentrated on the contents of the cabinets, and the only sound was the occasional shuffling of paper and the opening and closing of drawers.

Silver started at the top of the cabinet. She opened the drawer and began to look through the contents. The items were neatly organized and labeled. However, these appeared to be personal documents. She closed the top drawer, and began her way toward the bottom, but it became quickly apparent that these were not school related.

She knelt down on the floor to look through the bottom drawer and quickly had the same realization that she had about the contents of the other drawers.

To the right of the cabinet was a closet, its folding doors open a bit, revealing the inside. From where Silver was, however, she couldn't see much. She thought it was possible he had papers stored in there, so she peeked inside the doors, still on her knees.

The sound she heard from the inside made her jump backwards, getting the attention of everyone in the room.

"I guess you found Atticus," Dave said, turning around toward the closet.

Silver got a little bit closer and the cat hissed again from its position on the closet floor. Silver could now see the cat's body, tense and poised, still hissing at her.

"This must be the mean cat," Silver said as she got to her feet, glad to be putting some distance between her and Atticus.

"Not really," said Dave, as he turned back around to his file cabinet. The cat squeezed out of the opening in the closet doors, and scurried his way out of the room. Silver felt a little disappointed as he left, and wondered where the cat was that had rubbed up against her.

Just as Silver turned her thoughts back to searching for the exam, Karly turned around toward the middle of the room.

"I think I've got it," she said.

Every cell in Silver's body lit up and vibrated, as she made her way over to the desk where Karly had set down the manila folder.

"This is it, right?" Karly asked as Silver looked down at the contents of the folder.

The tab on the folder was labeled with their semester, but nothing else. It didn't matter.

There were about thirty handouts in the folder, each with seven questions on them and Final Exam listed at the top.

She looked over the questions and recognized a couple of them from the exam review they had received this morning in class.

On the left hand side of the folder was stapled the same paper with the same questions, but below each question were bullet points with a phrase or small sentence. This was it.

"Is that it, Silver?" Anthony asked, looking over her shoulder at the folder.

"Yep," Silver said feeling triumphant. "We only need one of these." She took one of the exams and folded it. Then put it in her back pocket.

"Wait, why don't you take one of the answer keys?" Anthony asked.

Silver flipped through the pile and saw only the exams. There was only one answer key.

"There's only one," she said, feeling disappointed.

"Here," Karly said as she opened the top right drawer, "give me the exam, I'll write down the answers."

Karly fished inside for a pen and found one, while Silver pulled the exam from her pocket and unfolded it, laying it on the desk for Karly to write on.

She watched as Karly began writing down the answers to each question, and for the first time in weeks began to feel something like peace. This had been so easy, and now she knew she would get an A in the class.

As she watched Karly write, a light source outside of the window illuminated the exam and she was momentarily glad that she could finally see better. Then it struck her.

Those were headlights.

CHAPTER 11

Outside the window, two beams of light lit up the grass as a car pulled into the driveway. A second later they were gone, and Silver heard a car door close.

"Hurry," Silver said to Karly who was still writing down the answers.

"Silver, we've got to get out of here," Mike said, panic in his voice.

"You guys go," Silver said to the three boys. They could hear the key in the lock. Silver hoped Mr. Bailey had a deadbolt on the front door.

Dave, Anthony, and Mike ran from the room and Silver could only assume they were going toward the back door where they had entered. She heard Mr. Bailey's key enter a second lock, and said a silent prayer of gratitude for the deadbolt. She heard the backdoor open and the scuffling of three large bodies trying to exit.

"I've got the first five. Let's go," Karly said, grabbing up the exam with the answers written on it and stuffing it into her back pocket.

Silver went for the window as she heard the front door open. She unlocked it and began to open it, praying it didn't have a screen. The cold air hit her body and she stuck her hand out into the night. No screen.

She knew he could hear them. There was no way that he couldn't. But it was too late now.

She wrenched the window up as high as it could go and swung one leg out of the window onto to the ground, then the other one until she was fully out of the house.

Surprisingly, she didn't run for the trees right away, but waited for Karly to get out of the house.

As soon as they were both out, they took off.

The thirty-foot sprint didn't take long, and relief washed over her as they both entered the cover of the trees. Silver turned around long enough to see Mr. Bailey at his open office window, looking out into the yard.

They had left the folder with the exams open on top of his desk, and his top right desk drawer open. There hadn't been any time. She hoped that one of the boys had locked the back door behind them, or it would be obvious who had been in his house.

The peace she had felt upon finding the exam had shattered, and the pieces fell behind her into the leaves and undergrowth so she felt that only part of her would make it to safety. They had messed up.

Once on the other side of the trees she felt marginally better, but her breathing was ragged and her heart rate massive. Despite the cold, she was sweating and felt much too warm. She ran up to Dave's back door and entered his house with Karly right behind her.

Dave, Anthony, and Mike were all standing around the kitchen table catching their breath. Dave looked at her and she hated what she saw in his expression.

"What happened?" Dave asked.

"We made it out, but he knew someone was in the house. He heard us."

"Did he see you?" Anthony asked.

"I don't think so," Silver said. "Karly, you were the last out. Did he see you?"

"I was outside before he came in the room," she said, her breathing heavy. "But I was only able to write down five of the answers."

Silver looked at her then and saw her bracelets. She hoped Mr. Bailey hadn't heard them as they left the house. That would be another clue as to who had been there.

"Were you guys able to lock the door?" Silver asked.

"Yeah," Dave said. "I made sure."

He still wore the key around his neck. He seemed to notice at the same time Silver did and lifted the leather string over his head and off his body. He hung it back up on the key ring. It swung back and forth as it settled into place among the other keys and yet to Silver it now stood out amongst the rest.

"The folder with the exams is still open on his desk. We didn't have time to put it away." Silver brought it up before anyone had the chance to ask her.

"The drawer was still open too," Karly said. The room went completely silent.

"He's going to know it had to have been students," Mike said. He fidgeted in place, his gaze locked on the floor. He grabbed hold of the back of one of the chairs and Silver noticed his arms shook a little.

"Yeah, and he'll think of me first because I have a key. Even though we locked the door, it's obvious no one had to break in," Dave said.

Silver felt guilty. She hadn't thought that if anything went wrong this would fall disproportionately on Dave. As long as Mr. Bailey hadn't actually seen the rest of them, he would never think that they had been in his house. But Dave would come to mind right away.

"Maybe he'll think the window was already open, and that's how we got in," Karly said.

"He doesn't leave windows open," Dave said, his voice soft and tired.

Silver couldn't look at him. Didn't want to. She racked her brain for an idea that would assuage her guilt. They needed something that would distract attention away from this event. Point Mr. Bailey in another direction. Something that wouldn't make him think of Dave first.

She thought back to the day when Dave had first caught her in Mr. Bailey's classroom after school. If he had never walked in that classroom, none of them would be here right now. Silver would have gone back to the other cheerleaders, and—

The spray paint. It was still in the trunk of her car.

A rush of thoughts and images came to her and before she was able to see the whole picture, she was speaking to the group.

"Guys, let's go to school," her energy was back. This would save all of them, and they would still have the exam.

"Go to school? We might be going to jail!" Mike said, slamming the chair forward into the table. "We've got to do something. We've got to get away from here."

"That's what we're doing," Silver said, feeling calm once again. "We're going to do something so we don't get in trouble for this."

Her voice had quieted, deepened, which had created a sharp contrast between Mike's panicked yells. They all looked at her and waited.

"We're going to create a distraction," she began, not taking any time to beat around the bush. "I have spray paint in my car. Let's go to school and use it. Create a bigger event. Maybe even something that will seem connected. Make what happened in Mr. Bailey's house look small. We're not the types to vandalize school property. They won't ever think of us."

All she heard was breathing.

"That's crazy," Dave said, but didn't seem to have any other objections.

"It's all we have," Silver said.

She wasn't only trying to make them follow her. She believed this, and it was the only thought her mind had room for at the moment. Silver didn't know what would happen if Mr. Bailey called the police, or if he had any idea of who had been in his house, or how they would be punished for this if they were caught, but she did know they absolutely, without a doubt, had to go to school and spray paint the walls. There were no other options. Only this.

"We're wasting time. We have to go," Silver said, knowing that she was wearing them down. "Does anyone else have any ideas?"

There was no response.

"Get in my car. We're only taking one."

The other four looked dazed, but did what she said. If anyone objected, they didn't voice it. They gathered coats and belongings in silence and walked out the door.

"How am I supposed to get back home?" Dave said as he stood by the car door waiting for Silver to open it.

"I'll bring you and Karly back," Silver said, and added as she heard Mike about to speak, "Mike, I'll drop you guys off at the house before I do. Anthony, take shotgun. Karly, get in the middle in the back."

Her car was a tight fit for all five of them, especially for three large male bodies. As she barked orders, her mind felt exceptionally clear.

Silver turned the key in the ignition and as the car came to life, she put the window all the way down, letting in the cold air. She was still warm.

The car zipped over country roads, much too fast for the dark twists and turns, which were so familiar to Silver in the daylight. She felt like they were on a ride at an amusement park, the feeling of being safely out of control thrilling and overwhelming. Her stomach seemingly falling every time there was a drop or sharp turn. She looked over at Anthony in the passenger seat, his window was also open. No one in the back was complaining about the cold air.

Silver pulled into the parking lot at school, like she had done so many times before, but this time she pulled right up to the front entrance, careful not to pull in front of the security camera.

She looked around. Hers was the only car there.

She turned the car off and got out, going toward the trunk where the spray paint was. She opened the trunk and saw the dozen or so cans of paint, and began handing them to the other four who were now huddled around her, waiting.

She was careful not to hand out the gold color, as that would be too obvious, but she did take the color red for herself. She wanted the red.

The last thing she pulled from her trunk was the club that she rarely used to lock the steering wheel of the car. She had always thought it was pretty useless as there weren't many places she need-ed it, but suddenly it had a purpose.

She handed it over to Anthony.

"Take out the camera first, then the door. There'll be an alarm, so we'll only have a few minutes."

Anthony stood with the club in his hand, and he reminded her of a caveman. The other three stood around not saying a word. Silver nodded.

Anthony wound up and brought the security camera crashing to the ground. He wound up once more and hit one of the front doors. Hundreds of little lines appeared on it, like a hundred spider webs competing for space. When he brought it down again, some of the glass fell onto the floor of the lobby and onto the concrete outside. The alarm sounded as he broke all the way through the door. One by one they entered the lobby, and went to work immediately.

Silver walked to the left and found an empty swath of wall, shook the can of paint and depressed the button on top. She watched the red lines, as if of their own will, and felt as if she was simply an observer in this situation. Not fully responsible for any of it.

She heard the metallic clinking of the cans being shaken, and the angry hiss of paint being released and was glad for it because it drowned out her thoughts.

Her only objective was to get as much paint on the wall as possible in a few short minutes before they had to leave. She was running out of space, and as she was looking for a fresh spot her eyes fell on the floor.

A second later, red marks appeared by her feet, she supposed of her own accord, but in her mind it was as if they rose up from somewhere deep in the earth. Like they had already been there all along and she was now just seeing them.

She heard something crash behind her and looked to see Mike overturn a trash can that was in his way. A few pieces of paper and some bottles rolled onto the floor as Mike continued to decorate his wall space, shaking the can vigorously every few seconds.

Silver looked around and was pleased to see the amount of paint on the walls, and was thinking to herself that they could leave any second now when the sound of more glass shattering caught her attention.

She whirled around to see Mike with the club in his hand smashing the trophy case to bits, glass flying and shelves breaking. Plaques and cups and trophies falling to the floor, some breaking in the process until no more destruction could be done.

Mike began picking up the items that had fallen from the case and throwing them down the hallways or back toward the front doors or wherever they went after leaving his hand.

Anthony rushed to restrain him, struggling against Mike's slightly smaller but still powerful body, and Silver realized that it was time to leave.

She yelled at the group to get back in the car, and Anthony had to forcefully push Mike, who still wanted to break things, toward the door. Finally he acquiesced and went back through the broken front door.

Karly and Dave followed behind Mike and Anthony, and Silver was the last one in the lobby.

She looked around for a few seconds at the red and black marks on the walls, the trash, glass, and plastic lying in pieces on the floor, and felt this was a job well done.

CHAPTER 12

Mike cried the entire way back to Silver's house. She sat in the driver's seat, window still all the way open, and became angrier and angrier at each one of Mike's sobs, softer and gentler than she would have imagined.

She didn't know what had happened to him back at the school, but was at least glad it had added to the vandalism.

She had to admit that she would never have thought of breaking the trophy case, but it had been a nice touch.

No one else said a word, and she certainly hadn't expected them to. This was no time for small talk and they didn't all know each other well enough to talk about anything real. Although, she supposed, they had certainly gotten to know each other better on this night.

Silver wished they never had to go to the school in the first place, that everything had gone smoothly at Mr. Bailey's, but it hadn't.

She felt pretty certain that this would at least throw Mr. Bailey and the police off Dave's trail. She wondered if they were at his house, examining the open window and the desk. Going through the house looking for clues as to who had been in it. It was obviously students at the school, no one else would be interested in an exam, and nothing else was missing or damaged.

At least they had the exam. With the answers. Karly still had it. Silver would make sure to get it from her before she left Dave's house. She would be the one to hold onto and distribute it. She simply didn't trust anyone else.

Finally, she pulled into her own driveway and Anthony and Mike got out without a word. No one else said a word either. Silver pulled away.

Ten minutes later they were back at Dave's house, getting out of the car. Karly went to leave.

"Wait. The exam," Silver said, holding out her hand.

"I can hang on to it," Karly said, not making any moves to pull it out of her pocket.

"No," Silver said, "I'm going to keep it. I'll get you a copy."

Karly didn't have much to negotiate with. Silver had organized the whole thing, and now that she had participated in the entire evening, she had nothing to hold over Silver's head. Her power had run out.

Karly reached in her back pocket and pulled out the folded exam. She handed it to Silver without a word.

"See you guys," she said, her bracelets jingling as she got back in the car. For once, the noise didn't irritate Silver.

"Let's see what's going on out back," Silver said, walking by Dave as she entered his house. He followed her in.

She walked into his bedroom and did not turn on the light. She twisted the rod that opened the blinds on his window, and the little slats parted, allowing her to see.

"You can't see his house from my house, remember? The trees," Dave said, standing in his bedroom doorway. The light from the living room back-lit him, making him look like all shadow.

"Let's go outside then. We can hide in the trees."

Dave looked exasperated but didn't say no to her.

They walked out the back door as they had earlier that evening, and walked toward the trees. This time without hurrying.

They reached the strip of trees and entered, leaves crunching beneath their feet. They walked in until the point when they could finally see Mr. Bailey's house and stopped, not wanting to go any further for fear of being seen. What Silver saw when she looked at his house surprised her.

Nothing was going on.

The house was dark, except for a light on somewhere in the house that peeked around the closed blinds. The office window had been closed, and the blinds in that room shut. It all seemed too peaceful.

"What's going on?" Silver said.

"From the looks of it, nothing," Dave said.

"Thanks," she said, giving him a look that said she had figured that much out for herself. "Shouldn't the police be here?"

"I don't know, Silver." His voice sounded tired, and she could tell he was losing patience with her.

"I don't understand. His house is all quiet."

"Maybe the police have already been here. Maybe he never called them. We don't know. What we have done, however, is made an even bigger mess of this night by vandalizing the school."

"I didn't hear any objections from you. Or anyone else."

Silver would have been angrier if she hadn't been so perplexed, and now she was getting nervous again. That Mr. Bailey may not have called the police made her more anxious than if she was looking at a house full of police officers right now.

"You're out of your mind," Dave said. She wasn't sure whether he expected a response to that or not.

"You followed me the whole way," Silver said, turning around and walking past Dave back toward his yard. There was nothing left to see here. She heard Dave behind her.

She walked back into his house, and was glad for the warmth and the light. Dave shut the door behind them.

"I've got to go," she said and he immediately looked disappointed.

"Where are you going?"

"What does it matter to you? And anyways, you told me I was crazy not three minutes ago. I assumed you were ready for me to leave."

He didn't say anything back, just stood there with an expression on his face Silver couldn't read.

"I've got to go somewhere to dump that stuff. I can't ride around with it. Not anymore."

"Where are you going to go?"

"I don't know. I'll figure something out."

"I'll come with you. I know a place."

Though she was glad for the offer of company, she paused here not knowing exactly what to say to him. Finally, she just said what she was thinking.

"Are you angry with me or not? Because I can't read you right now."

Dave looked at her, then looked away, then back again. On the last time, he held her gaze like he wanted to tell her something that was going to take him a long time. She stared back at him, unmoving.

"Yes," he stared back at her. "No."

Silver was now exasperated, yet also charged by their back and forth.

"Okay, you're too complicated. If you're coming with me, get in the car."

"I'm too complicated?" Dave said before Silver shushed him on her way out the door.

Dave stepped outside a few seconds later with a flashlight in hand.

"Probably will need this," he said, holding it up as he walked back into the carport. "And this," he held out a shovel as he walked toward her car.

They both got back in Silver's car, and rolled their windows down again. Only partway this time. It felt weird to have Dave riding beside her, but nice too. Soothing after the insanity of the evening.

"Okay, where are we going?"

"At the end of my street, take a right." Silver did as she was told.

They rode a minute in silence, the wind whipping through the car and Silver finally feeling a little chilly. She rolled her window back up. Dave kept his down.

"What does your mom do that she works so late?" Silver asked, suddenly curious.

"She's a bartender," Dave said.

"Really?" This was not the answer Silver was expecting.

"Pays the bills," Dave said with a shrug.

"So is she gone like this every night? You're always here by yourself?"

"Well, like four nights a week. Definitely on the weekends."

"Hmm." She considered this, and thought it seemed like he spent a lot of time alone.

"Do you ever see your dad?"

"No, not really."

Dave didn't offer any more information, but Silver decided to press on.

"Why not?" she asked.

Dave was looking out the window, letting the wind blow in his face. He didn't turn toward her as he answered.

"He left when I was five. He pops up now and again, but I never count on it. He doesn't live in this state."

"Do you have any brothers or sisters?"

"Nope, just me."

"Do you wish you did?"

"Do I wish what? That I saw my dad or that I had brothers and sisters?"

"Either."

"Yeah, probably. And, maybe."

Silver thought she heard him sigh, but it could have just been the wind. He still faced the window.

"Why do you wear that jacket every day?"

Now he turned to face her.

"Could I ask a few questions?"

"Yes, after you answer this one." She took her eyes off the road and turned toward him, smiling. He actually smiled back at her.

"I don't know. I like it."

"But it's denim, and there's a hand-drawn dragon on the back."

"So?"

"So? Dave," Silver took a breath like she was preparing for a big speech, "do you know how that makes you look to other people? It's weird, and people stay away from you because of it. I mean, I like you," she saw him glance at her quickly," but, before you ever cornered me in Mr. Bailey's classroom," she glanced at him, "I didn't know what to think. I kept thinking to myself, who draws a dragon on the back of their jacket and then wears it every day? If we hadn't had our chance encounter, I would have never spoken to you. Something about that jacket just says 'Don't speak to me.'"

It was silent for a few seconds in the car, and Silver worried that she had offended him. She hadn't meant to be mean, just honest, which in her opinion, was the biggest gesture of friendship she could offer him

"So, you like me, huh?" Dave had turned back toward the window.

Silver looked over at him, but couldn't get him to turn back toward her. Finally, she just turned her eyes back to the road.

"Yeah. Yeah, I do." She waited for his response.

"Wish I could say the same for you."

She was startled at first, but then noticed he was smiling. It was a little hard to see because his head was turned. She punched him in the shoulder.

"Ow," Dave said, rubbing the spot where she had hit him. "I'd hit you back, but I don't want you to crash the car."

Silver laughed, but didn't look back at him. She could tell he was looking at her though. She was surprised to hear him speak again.

"Yeah, I like you too."

Calm settled over the car, and the last of Silver's anxiety left her. At least for a little while.

"So, I never understood this. Are you and Anthony twins?"

This was a question she hadn't gotten in a while. Most people at school knew the answer, but it was a little confusing for people who didn't know them.

"No. He's thirteen months older than I am, but he has a late birthday so when it was time for him to start school, he waited a year, and we both started school at the same time."

"But you must have an even later birthday, why didn't you wait a year?"

"I don't know. My parents put us in school at the same time."

"An overachiever even in kindergarten."

He was making fun of her, but she didn't mind. It was true. She shrugged her shoulders and looked over at him, giving him a look that said "you're right" and "so what?" all at the same time.

"So when's your birthday?" he asked.

"October 10th."

"Interesting, mine is June 10th."

"Oooh, Gemini," Silver said, her mind wandering to everything she knew about Geminis, adding it to her mental picture of Dave as a person.

"You don't really believe in that stuff, do you?"

"This coming from someone who spends a lot of his time painting and reading about dragons. Yes, I believe in that stuff. Haven't you ever read a description of your sun sign and thought, wow, that actually describes me."

"I don't think I've ever read a description of my sun sign."

She looked over at him, squinting her eyes and tilting her head in disbelief, as if he had told her he had never looked in the mirror.

She turned her full attention back to the road for a moment. As they continued to wind their way down it, she wondered how much longer they had to go to get to Dave's spot.

"How much longer is it until we get to this place?" she asked.

"Actually, it's right up ahead. See that road up on the right? Turn there."

Silver looked ahead and saw a street sign that her headlights had caught. It was a residential street like Dave's. She pulled onto it and waited for more instructions.

"Okay, keep going down. I'll tell you when to stop."

They rode by maybe ten houses on either side until finally the street came to a dead end. It was really dark down here as they had left the streetlights a few houses back. She stopped the car and killed the engine.

"This is either a really good place to hide the spray paint or you're going to kill me out here and leave my body."

"Yeah, I haven't decided which yet," Dave said, playing along.

They got out of the car and opened the trunk. Silver grabbed the bag of spray paint. Dave grabbed the shovel and checked to see that he still had the flashlight on him.

"I'm at your mercy," Silver said, turning toward him to follow his lead.

"Those words have a nice ring in my ears," Dave said, smiling as he began walking. They were entering the woods for real this time, not just a patch of trees that separated two yards.

"I'm afraid to ask, but how do you know about this place?" Silver asked, the bag of paint she carried hitting her thighs as she walked.

"We used to live on this street. My house was on the left a few houses in as we came down the street. All the neighborhood kids, we would play in these woods. Try to build forts and stuff, collect tadpoles, you know, all that kind of stuff."

Silver didn't know. She didn't think she had ever spent any extended time out in nature, certainly not playing in the forest. Frankly, even in the daylight, she would probably be a little afraid to be here. She didn't like that there was stuff she couldn't see that might touch her.

Dave walked on her right, his jacket on but unbuttoned, another black T-shirt underneath, and the shovel in his right hand. For some reason, she liked the way he carried the shovel, gripping its handle firmly in his hand, easily holding its weight.

"Cool," she said, not really having any reply to his comment about playing in the woods.

"We don't have to go too much farther."

The flashlight illuminated their way enough so that they could move forward at a reasonable pace. Dave held it in his left hand shining it down on the path in front of them.

"Are you left handed?" Silver asked.

"Yeah," Dave said, then stopped abruptly. "Here we are."

Silver wondered what made this spot different from all the places in here. To her it was the same as everywhere else—trees and dead leaves.

"Okay," she said as she set the bag of paint down.

Dave began to dig a hole, slamming the shovel into the ground and placing the dirt to his left. Silver watched him closely, admiring his physical presence.

"I can do that, you know. It's my garbage we're burying."

"Yeah, you probably should be doing this. But if I do it, it'll get done faster," Dave said as he continued to dig.

Silver stood around and watched, holding the flashlight over the hole Dave was digging. She listened to the sounds around her. The shovel hitting the earth, the loose dirt falling into a pile, an insect, the leaves being disturbed—either by the wind or maybe a small animal—and found herself enjoying the sensations. Nothing to do, nothing to see, just the sounds around her.

Dave finished digging and looked at her, and she placed the bag with all the paint into the ground.

Not very environmentally friendly, she thought with some sadness as she realized that the cans still had a lot of paint in them.

Dave just looked at her and shook his head. He was smiling though.

Silver took the shovel from him so she could cover the bag with the dirt. This part she could at least do.

Finally, it was completely covered and she was rid of it. Yet, oddly, she felt worse than she had before.

Dave bent down to the spot and covered it with the dead leaves around them so no one could tell anything had been buried there. When he was done, it looked like they had never been there.

Neither of them moved to turn back toward the car.

Silver bent down to the earth over the spot where the paint was and swished her hand through the leaves that Dave had scattered on top. Not to check that it was done properly, just to say good-bye.

"So what is this spot?" she asked Dave while standing up.

Dave turned away from her and put his hand on a tree with a thick trunk, running his fingers over the bark.

"This was my spot," he said, then looked up. "I used to climb this tree. I would come here by myself, without the other kids around."

He put his hand on a thick branch that was fairly low, and Silver got the impression that he was remembering himself getting up on it.

"Let's climb it," Silver said as she walked over to the tree and put her own hands on it. She liked the feeling of the rough bark on her skin.

"Seriously?"

"Yeah. You can still do it, right?"

"Well, I'm a little bigger than I was when I was eight, but probably." Dave looked up, judging if he could still climb the tree. "Why don't you go first? I'll help you up."

Silver positioned herself in front of the low branches, grabbing a hold of one she could get her hands on. Dave formed his hands into a step and Silver put her foot in them and hoisted herself up. Finally, she got her feet firmly onto the lowest branch and started to climb.

She went up into the tree several more levels, and stopped as the branches became thinner and less reliable looking. She sat down where she stopped, holding onto another branch to steady herself, and looked down.

Dave was making his way up. He climbed to about where she was, a little lower, and sat down.

"That's where I used to sit," he said, indicating where she was.

"Really?" she said. He nodded.

It was cold, but not uncomfortably so. Silver sat in the tree looking out from her branch and thought to herself what a strange night this had been. By now someone had seen what they had done. She wondered what would happen in the morning, but figured she would cross that bridge when she came to it.

As long as she was in the tree she didn't have to deal with it. They both sat there for a few minutes not saying anything, until finally it was time to get down.

Dave went first, making his way through the branches. He was all the way down before Silver began her descent. As her feet touched the lowest branch, Dave put his arms up to her and without asking, grabbed her around the waist and lifted her out of the tree.

With her feet firmly on the earth and his arms still around her, she turned toward him and put her arms around his torso underneath his jacket so she touched his T-shirt. He pulled her closer and she was surprised how warm he was, given the cold weather. She hesitated to pull away, but when she did, she looked up at him.

"Thank you," she said.

"You're welcome."

Dave picked up the shovel and they both walked away.

CHAPTER 13

When she got home, Anthony was already in bed even though it wasn't very late. The house was quiet and she wished for more noise, more activity. She put her keys down on the table where she always put them and walked into the living room, flipping on the TV to kill the silence.

She sat down and didn't know what to do. She wasn't tired, but there was nothing left that needed to be done. Well, there was one thing actually.

She walked upstairs, hearing the noise from the TV get fainter as she went and walked into the office where the computer and printer were.

She pulled out the folded piece of paper from her back pocket with the typed questions and five handwritten answers on it, and looked at it for a moment. She realized she would need to tell everyone not to only answer the five questions there were answers for. Everyone should pick at least one of the questions that didn't have an answer. Still though, they had more than they needed for a good exam grade.

Silver had what she wanted. She could memorize these questions and answers and walk into the exam completely confident. She thought this would make her feel safe, peaceful, and yet something still nagged at her.

She put the paper face down on the printer's surface and made four copies, being careful not to make any more than they needed.

To be honest, the person she was most worried about showing someone else or losing it was Anthony. At least he lived in her house and she could keep an eye on him. Everyone else would do what they needed to do to keep this safe.

Finally, she had her copies and there was nothing left to do.

* * *

Silver lay awake in bed that night, alternately tossing one way and then another. She was hot, she was cold, she was thirsty. Whatever it was, she couldn't sleep.

She threw the blankets off of her, letting them bunch at the end of her bed and stared up at the ceiling.

She kept thinking about what would happen in the morning. She guessed that everything had gone all right, at least after they had made it back from the school, and yet she dreaded what she might find out.

She felt bad. They had trashed the school lobby, and she really hadn't meant to do that.

Someone would have to clean that up, pay money to get stuff fixed. No one would be able to walk in and out of there for days.

She had buried paint in the ground, some of those cans pretty full. She imagined the paint leaking out and into the ground, contaminating the things around it. Killing stuff, maybe. She didn't want to be a killer.

And Mr. Bailey. Why had it seemed like he hadn't done anything after he found them in his house? This was what worried her the most. What was he thinking? Did he know it was them? Was he playing some kind of game with her?

She would see him first thing tomorrow morning. She hadn't thought of that. She hadn't thought of a lot of things.

She envied Anthony his sleep, but once again, her brother had seemingly put everything out of his mind and had found his peace. She wondered if Mike was up like she was.

She wanted to call Dave, just to hear someone's voice. But he was asleep, and she had imposed on him enough already. She'd have to just endure by herself tonight.

She got up and walked to her window, pulling the blinds up and for some reason looked for the moon, even though she hadn't seen it all night. She didn't see it here either. It had to be new.

Silver unlocked the window and opened it several inches, letting in the winter air. This was the only way she was going to sleep.

She got back in bed and pulled the blankets up again, this time feeling the cold air on her face and she started to calm down. As the temperature dropped in her room, she got more comfortable and sleepier and finally she realized that when she woke up it would be time to face the daylight.

CHAPTER 14

Silver admitted to herself that it looked worse in the daylight.

She pretended to be shocked at the destruction just like everyone else, but in reality she wasn't sure what she was feeling.

She felt a little bit like she was on autopilot, her body moving, she just wasn't sure how. She certainly wasn't giving it any instructions.

Seeing the police here scared her. She hadn't really thought about the legal ramifications of their actions last night. She had been so focused on getting that exam.

She looked down at her hands again, sure she had paint and dirt all over them. That someone would notice and she would get arrested and instead of spending the day in school, she would spend the day sitting in jail.

She needed some water and fresh air would be nice too, but she was already inside and had to get to class. She didn't want to go back out.

She walked to the water fountain nearby and gulped down some water, feeling marginally better. She couldn't believe that she had to go sit in Mr. Bailey's class right now. She wondered if he was going to say anything about last night. He must have reported it by now. But maybe not. She couldn't ask about it. She wasn't supposed to know it even happened.

She had brought the exam copies with her today to give to the others. They were in her bag right now. Suddenly, she realized that was insane. She could have found some other way to get them to people.

She reached the door to her classroom, and had no choice but to enter.

Mr. Bailey sat at his desk, looking busy and serious as usual. Her classmates chatted and walked around. Dave was reading at his desk, Mike waved hello to her. Anthony and Karly weren't there yet. Totally normal. It freaked her out.

She didn't know how she was going to make eye contact with Mr. Bailey. But she had to. It would look suspicious otherwise. She hadn't noticed Karly walk in, but suddenly she was in her seat. The bell rang and Anthony slipped in the door. Class had begun.

Mr. Bailey stood up, walked to the front of the class and began talking. Silver could barely focus on what he was saying, she was so worried about making or not making eye contact. He probably thought something was wrong with her eyes.

She waited for him to mention something, anything, about last night. Start accusing people. Intimidate them into talking. Instead, he just talked about *Catcher in the Rye*.

She should feel great. It was looking like they had actually gotten away with stealing the exam, not to mention vandalizing the school, but she couldn't shake the feeling that something wasn't right.

Silver looked around at the others, to see if they were reacting to this, but everyone looked like they always did. She didn't get it.

Finally, there was nothing left for her to do other than to sit back and try to listen as best she could. This was going to be a long week.

* * *

At three o'clock that afternoon, Silver entered the art room. She had the thought that she might as well grab a canvas and some paint and make something, she was in here so much.

The truth was that she needed to give Dave his copy of the exam, but the other part of the truth is that she just wanted to talk to him. Also, she thought there was a decent chance of Karly being here, and the both of them being alone, which would allow her to kill two birds with one stone.

She had already given Mike his copy. He took it from her with barely a word, and he didn't look very good. Certainly wasn't very cheerful. She hoped nothing was wrong. That would be her fault too.

She realized too late in the day that, of course, she hadn't needed to bring Anthony's copy to school, she could just give it to him at home. So she held onto it. At least that would prevent him from showing someone, or God forbid, making copies and trying to sell them or something.

Dave was in his usual chair, working away. When he heard someone enter the room, he turned around and actually looked pleased to see her. This, Silver thought, was a good sign, but, honestly, she couldn't believe he still wanted anything to do with her.

"Hey," she said, to him, then mouthed, "are you alone?"

"Yeah," he said, putting down his brush. "What's going on?"

"I have something for you," she said, without mentioning what it was or outright handing it to him. She didn't have to explain.

"Okay, cool," he said, neither having to ask what it was or expecting it immediately.

She didn't know quite what to say, but wanted to say something. She wished he would start talking, but he just sat there looking at her in his white T-shirt and jeans.

"Switching it up with the white T-shirt today instead of the black. Nice."

"Yeah, you know, I could maybe do green, maybe blue, but it's just simpler with black and white," he smiled at her, at ease with her teasing. "Looks best with the jacket too."

"You better keep a close eye on that thing, because if I get my hands on it, I'm gonna burn it."

"You'd owe me a jacket then."

"I would love to buy you a new jacket," Silver said in all seriousness.

Dave just laughed and shook his head.

Silver moved from where she was standing and sat on the table next to where Dave was, putting her feet on the stool in front of her. He waited for her to speak.

"It looks bad," she began, not needing to say what.

"Yeah," he said, pausing, "Mike went nuts last night."

Silver gestured with her hands emphatically that meant "I know," and let Dave continue speaking.

"I was right next to him and I thought when he knocked that trash can over that he had accidentally bumped into it. But then, all of the sudden, he's smashing everything to pieces, and throwing trophies down the hallway." Dave rubbed at his temple with his left hand. "I'm not sure what put him over the edge."

Silver thought about Mike and felt guilty that she had dragged him into all this. But it was too late now.

"I didn't really mean for that to happen," she said, surprised that she was expressing this thought. "That's not what I intended. I feel like," she paused trying to choose her words, "everything got out of control last night, and I couldn't stop it. I thought I," she paused once more, "had it all figured out."

Dave didn't reply immediately, but Silver wished he would. Wished that he would say something that would make sense and would make her feel better.

"Things don't always go as planned. And with what we were trying to pull off, we should be grateful even more things didn't go wrong."

She didn't know if that made sense or if it made her feel better, but suddenly she had a burning curiosity to ask him something.

"Why did you agree to this? Anthony and Mike, I knew I could persuade them. Karly muscled me into coming along. But, you, you're smarter than all of this. So why?"

Dave stood up. Walked to the window and tinkered around with some stuff sitting on the ledge. He turned around and looked at her, and she felt that same feeling she had before, like being pulled toward him.

"You offered me something and we made a deal. That's why."

"You're lying," Silver said, getting up from the table and walking toward him. "Why did you really come along?"

She saw him swallow and look off and up to his right. She knew he wouldn't lie to her this time.

"Because ..." he took a deep breath," because I just wanted to follow you."

That wasn't what she had been expecting.

"Why?" she asked, genuinely curious.

Dave looked off again, and shook his head.

"I don't know. I just felt ... drawn."

Silver considered this thought and didn't quite know what it meant. It didn't make her feel better or worse, and unfortunately, didn't quite satisfy her curiosity as to his motives. She went and sat next to him by the window, pulling herself up to the table that ran along it, and seating herself on top.

"What does that mean?" she asked.

"People want to follow you. For better or worse, I guess."

Silver had never thought about that before. Granted, she was in charge of a lot of stuff, and she guessed she had never had trouble persuading others to do what she wanted, but she had never given thought to why that was.

"So, where did I lead us?"

"I think we have yet to find out."

She thought about this and felt afraid, because it meant that this situation was far from over. And she had a feeling that things were going to get worse before they got better.

"I have what I want," she said, making direct eye contact with him, "but I still don't feel right. We've gotten away with everything that we pulled last night, but, now, more than ever, I feel like I'm constantly looking over my shoulder."

She waited for him to respond, wanted him to say something, but he didn't. He just looked at her.

"I don't know what to say," Dave said after a minute.

"Do you think less of me?" Silver asked, finally getting to what was really on her mind.

"I don't think that's the question you're really asking," Dave said.

Silver immediately felt that he was right, but wasn't sure exactly what he was getting at.

She had nothing left to say, and felt like he didn't either. She wanted something from him, but she wasn't sure what. She wanted to be close to him, to touch him, for him to touch her, but felt like she might contaminate him. She felt too desperate, and knew that she just needed to get out of there.

She hopped down off the table, feeling restless, and pulled herself away from Dave, even though she didn't want to.

She walked over to her bag and grabbed a piece of paper out of it, folded it up and handed it to him.

"Keep it safe," she said, smiling, even though she didn't feel like it.

"Thanks," Dave said, not looking entirely happy. "So, is this it?" he asked her.

"What else is there?"

He walked away from the window and came toward her, getting very close. She stood there waiting, not backing away, but not getting any closer. He made no moves.

She made herself stay still, feeling like she might devour him if she got any closer. It was one thing if he came toward her, but if she moved toward him, she was worried he wouldn't survive the encounter.

Finally, she backed away, leaving him in his spot, and knew that she had to get away.

"I'll talk to you later?" she said.

"Yeah," he said, putting his hands into his front pockets.

She dragged herself away, not looking back.

* * *

Silver needed to get Karly her copy of the exam. She didn't really like the girl, and, certainly, had not forgiven her for blackmailing her way into the group, but she owed her this exam. Silver would make sure she got it.

It was Friday afternoon after school, and Silver was surprised that Karly hadn't sought her out yet.

Aside from seeing her in Mr. Bailey's class, she was nowhere to be found. Without her they would have only the questions, no answers, and Silver felt it was only honorable to make sure Karly got her copy.

Things had calmed down at school. The lobby had been cleaned up as much as possible, though there was still some paint on the walls and the floor, and the trophy case hadn't been replaced yet.

They had roped it off with that yellow crime-scene tape, which made her nervous every time she walked by.

She hadn't heard anything about who they suspected. It wasn't that far-fetched that some disgruntled student from past or present had vandalized the school. She still felt weird when she realized that it had been her.

She had heard absolutely nothing about Mr. Bailey's house. He apparently was keeping this secret. She had been checking the police blotter in the local paper. No mention. As far as she knew, in this moment, they were home free.

Silver stepped outside into the cold air and buttoned up her jacket to walk to her car. As she had her hand on the door handle, she heard the familiar sound of metal clinking against metal and looked around.

Five or six cars away, she saw Karly getting into her car, trying to fit a bunch of different art projects into it, putting one of them on top of the car as she pushed up the passenger side front seat to access the back of the car. Silver walked over.

"Need some help?"

Karly jumped and looked surprised to see who it was.

"Will you get on the side of the car and help me position it into the backseat? I need to fit this one in too." She motioned to the top of her car.

Silver walked over to the driver's side and helped her maneuver the art work. When they were done, Karly grabbed the piece that was on top and put that in.

"I've got your copy," Silver said. "I'm surprised you didn't come looking for it before now."

Karly started fiddling with something in the car, but Silver couldn't see what.

"I knew you had it, and I'd get it eventually."

"You were the one who almost got caught in the house, and without you, we wouldn't have the answers. You're the one who most deserves it."

"Yeah, you know, it's only a test. I'd do fine in the class without it. It's not the biggest deal in the world."

Silver reared back a little. If she hadn't cared about the grade, why had she made such a big deal about coming with them? She had gone to the trouble of blackmail, and now she suddenly didn't care that much?

"I don't understand," Silver came right out with it, "if it's not that big of a deal to you, then why did you twist my arm to come with us? You had me cornered in the art room, at your mercy. It sure seemed to me that you cared about this exam."

Karly looked at Silver, then reached into her bag to grab her sunglasses. She put them on and looked back at Silver, this time with hidden eyes, and Silver got the impression that Karly was suddenly intimidated by her again.

"I don't know. I overheard you guys and took the opportunity I had. Honestly, I never would have been that worried about it if I hadn't heard you guys, but I just thought ..."

Karly stopped, looking at the ground and fidgeting around. She put her hand on her hips and looked off to her right.

"You thought what?" Silver asked, not one kind note in her tone of voice.

"I thought that ... I thought that it would be nice to be more powerful than you for a moment."

Silver didn't know what to think. She wasn't angry, or hurt, or sympathetic. Just confused.

Karly fidgeted some more on her side of the car, and it made her jewelry clink together.

"You wanted more power than me," Silver repeated, not as a question, just as a statement. "But we could have gotten caught, we could have gotten in trouble, and you don't even care about the exam grade? You just wanted to one up me? That's crazy."

Karly laughed, and Silver was getting tired of people who all seemed to be in on the joke except for her.

"Is it?" Karly asked. "Silver, you're good at a lot of things, but the thing is, you suffer from a complete lack of self-awareness."

Silver didn't exactly feel insulted, but she also didn't think Karly had meant this as a compliment.

"Okay. What's that supposed to mean?"

"It's funny. I always thought you knew exactly where you were going, and now I know that you haven't got a clue what you actually want. In fact, that's the best thing I got out of this whole experience."

Karly held her hand out to Silver, indicating that she wanted the exam. Silver walked around the car and handed it to her.

"Still nice to have, even though it really doesn't matter for me either way," Karly said.

"Yeah, well, thanks," Silver said, feeling unsure of herself suddenly.

Karly walked around to the driver's side and started to get into her car, and Silver walked back toward hers.

"Hey," Karly yelled over to her as Silver reached her car, "I hope you find what you're looking for someday. Really."

Silver, not in the mood for any more riddles or puzzles, kind of nodded her head in Karly's direction, hoping to have nothing else to do with this girl for the rest of her life. She got into her car and assumed that Karly drove off. She didn't look to find out.

* * *

When Silver got home ten minutes later, she entered what she assumed was an empty house. Her parents were still away, and Anthony would be at practice.

She threw her keys and her bag down, and walked into the living room, flopping down on the couch. She looked out the window, but didn't really watch anything. She was too busy thinking about the things Dave and Karly had said to her.

Usually, she felt better informed and more clear-headed than everyone else and now she felt like the complete opposite. She lay there feeling sorry for herself for a few minutes, before she heard heavy footsteps coming down the stairs.

"Hey," Anthony said, as he bounced down the stairs.

"What are you doing home?" Silver asked, looking up, but not getting up from the couch.

"Practice ended early. Coach had to take one of his kids some-where. So we just had a short meeting and then left. Mike dropped me off."

"How is he, by the way?" Silver asked. She had felt a little wor-ried about Mike in the last couple of days. More so than anyone else.

"Fine, I guess," Anthony said, not seeming to have much to say or really any opinion on the subject.

"That's good," Silver said, laying her head back down.

"What's with you? I thought you'd be bouncing with joy con-sidering the events of the last couple of days. You did it, right? You pulled this all off. Now, you're home free."

She envied her brother's simplicity more than ever in this mo-ment. She wished she could feel like that.

"I don't know. Maybe I just have leftover nerves from the other night, or something."

"Well, whatever it is, I'm sure you'll feel great when you walk into the exam knowing that you will totally ace it. I know I will."

"I thought we talked about you getting a B on this exam."

Anthony getting an A with near perfect answers would defi-nitely look suspicious. And she had to remember that even if he wasn't telling anyone about it, Mr. Bailey knew someone had been in his house looking at those exams.

"Yeah, exactly. I know what to do," Anthony said as he walked into the kitchen and began pulling out items from the fridge to make a sandwich with. He would eat three of them.

Silver had too much energy, she needed to do something.

"I'm going to get on the treadmill," she said, as she hopped off the couch and started up the stairs to change clothes.

Anthony nodded back at her, his mouth full of lunchmeat.

A few minutes later, Silver was in the basement, running at a steady pace with her earbuds in. She was already breaking a sweat. The exertion felt good to her restless body.

Her feet pounded the rubber of the treadmill and her arms pumped back and forth to the rhythm of her gait. She should really join the track team, she thought. Then she might not get into so much trouble.

Five minutes went by, then ten, then fifteen. The more she ran, the more her mind cleared, until she felt like she was thinking normally again. Somewhere around twenty-three minutes, it hit her.

Something wasn't right.

She wasn't sure what it was, but something about the events of the prior few weeks had thrown something off. Granted, she had committed no less than two crimes, and had dragged along four people with her, but it was only just dawning on her that she couldn't live like this.

She needed to do something to set this right. She needed to fix this.

The first thought that popped into her mind was Dave. She needed to go see Dave. Tonight. Hopefully his mom was working.

She ran about ten minutes longer, feeling good about her decision. She wasn't sure exactly what she needed to say or do, but she needed to start with Dave.

* * *

She pulled up to his house, this time familiar with his street and driveway and walked up to his front door. She almost went in without knocking, but figured she'd be polite.

She had texted him about a half hour ago to tell him she was stopping by. His only response had been "OK." She couldn't tell if that was good or bad.

She heard the locks click behind the door and then Dave was standing in front of her.

"Will you ever leave me alone?" he said, a hint of a smile on his face.

She pushed past him into the house and felt better about her decision to come over.

She could smell food, like someone had just cooked dinner. But when she looked into the kitchen it was all clean, not a pot or fork anywhere on the counters or in the sink.

"Did you cook?" she asked, not bothering to hide her shock.

"Yeah, I made some chicken," Dave said, with a tone of voice that said he couldn't figure out why she was so amazed by this.

"And then you cleaned up?"

"Yes," Dave said, "I'm the only one here. Who else is going to do it?"

Silver just stood there alternately staring at the kitchen and looking back at Dave. She took off her coat and draped it across one of the kitchen table chairs. As she did so, she noticed the key to Mr. Bailey's house hanging on the key hook. She turned her attention away quickly.

"I'm the only one home a lot of nights. If I don't cook, I don't eat. And if I don't clean up, well, that's just gross. Not to mention my mom would be pissed when she got home."

"Makes sense," Silver said, "if I had known you were cooking I would have texted you earlier."

"What makes you think I'd cook dinner for you?"

"My charming personality and delightful company."

Dave laughed. "Yeah, I don't even know what to say to that."

Silver walked into the living room and made herself at home on the couch. The TV was turned to some dumb reality TV show, which she immediately got sucked into.

"Are you watching this?" she asked.

"You know, you're always the one with all the questions. This is my house. And you're in my seat," he said sitting down on the other end of the couch, but not asking her to move. "No, I'm not watching this. When I turned the TV on this is the channel that was on. I was interrupted by a knock on the door before I could change it."

"Likely story," Silver said, pushing his thigh with her foot. He grabbed her foot and pushed it back toward her.

"You're starting to learn," she said and laughed.

"Yeah, I've got to play rough with you."

They watched the TV for a few minutes, taking in the drama of the people on the show, keenly aware of each other's presence. Silver sat with her knees bent and feet up on the couch, and Dave sat with his feet propped up on the coffee table. She had never seen him without shoes before and seeing him in just socks was sort of funny to her. He was always in boots or something.

"Wow, this is amazing," Dave said in response to the TV.

"You like it," Silver said, almost kicking him again and then deciding not to. "I mean, how could you not. Do you know how much human nature, real human nature, you can observe by watching a show like this? If you can tune out the drunken fights and the drunken hook ups, you can actually learn something about people."

"Like what, how to become a crying, sloppy mess and impose on all of your friends when you're wasted? Or how to say over and over again to everybody that you're not going to cheat on your girlfriend back home, but then hook up with someone the first chance you get?"

"I said you have to look beyond that."

They stopped talking again and allowed the people on TV to be the only sound in the room. Silver felt like this was her opportunity. She still didn't know what she wanted to say.

"Dave?" Her voice was so gentle as to be unrecognizable. He looked at her with a fearful expression, as if she might tell him she had cancer or something.

"Yeah?"

"I have something I need to tell you."

She crossed her legs underneath her, and grabbed the remote to mute the TV. He turned his body toward her, feet still propped up on the table. For once, she had no words readily available.

"Um, okay ... I wanted to ... apologize."

She hadn't planned for that word to come out of her mouth, but it was the one that most wanted to.

"This has been crazy. These last few weeks. And that's my fault. But, that's not exactly what I wanted to say."

She paused again, and looked up at him quickly, as her eyes had been focused on her hands. He still looked shocked.

"When I ... started this whole thing ... I knew I needed you to come along. And I was going to do whatever it took."

She made eye contact with him and he stared right back at her.

"But, okay, I guess what I'm trying to say is that," her words came out slow and stunted, "I was going to use you for whatever I needed you for and discard you when I was done."

Dave fidgeted in his place on the couch and looked down at his lap.

"I just wanted to say I'm sorry ... That's a terrible way to treat people."

She had tears in her eyes, though there was really no threat of them spilling over.

"For what it's worth, and I realize that this might be the last few minutes of our friendship, I like you, and ... that's why I needed to tell you this and apologize."

Dave just sat and stared at her. And she stared back. She didn't want to start talking again and mess things up even further. She would just let him respond.

He pulled his feet off the table and put them on the carpet. He leaned forward resting his elbows on his knees.

Silver was honestly surprised that he hadn't kicked her out of his house yet. After a minute or so of just sitting there, she decided it was time for her to leave. She unwound her legs from underneath her and started to get up off the couch.

"Wait."

She stopped and turned around to look at him.

"Sit back down."

Now he was the one giving orders, she thought. She sat back down on the sofa, turning toward him with one leg up on the seat.

"I have to apologize too."

Silver was amazed. She waited for Dave to go on, and felt just a little bit better about being here still.

"I thought ... It felt good to know that I sort of had you under my thumb. That you needed me. I knew I had you."

Now she stared back at him.

"You had never even spoken to me before, maybe never even looked at me, and suddenly I had what you wanted. That felt good, and I was going to play that up for all it was worth."

"Did you really want to go to prom with me?"

"Yeah, because I wanted everyone to see that I had you, but mostly because I knew you hated the idea and had no choice."

She felt like she should be angry at this, and yet what she felt was something like empathy. This was language she understood, and her usual vindictiveness melted away underneath Dave's honest words.

"Do you still want to go?" she asked.

"We don't have to if you don't want to ... that was just some deal we made with each other. Nothing more than a transaction."

"That's not what I asked."

Silver moved closer to him, draping an arm over the back of the couch and folding her legs up in front of her.

Dave turned toward her also, mirroring her body position.

"Yeah. Do you?" he asked quickly.

"Yeah," Silver said, while nodding her head. "But we should do this right this time. Ask me."

"Why do I have to be the one to ask?"

"Well, I could do it too. But one of us has to ask. Do you want me to ask?"

"No, no. I'll ask."

He took a deep breath. She couldn't figure out why. He knew she would say yes.

"Do you want to go to prom with me?"

Silver looked back at him and couldn't help but think what a strange turn of events this was.

"Yes, I'd love to."

"That feels better," Dave said.

"Yeah, it does."

Neither of them knew what to do next or exactly what had happened, but they both sat on the couch, trying neither to overpower nor outdo the other one.

He started to move closer to her, but hesitated, pulling back at the last second. She was tired of waiting.

"Come here," she said as she scooted closer to him, sitting up on her knees and getting close to him. She was surprised at how warm his mouth was. She had the sensation of the heat being transferred to her.

He held back a little at first, not letting anything but his mouth touch hers, but then she felt his hand go around her waist.

She opened her mouth a little, and as she did so their kissing deepened and became more passionate, which she was more than ready for.

Just as she was starting to wonder where this was going, he pulled her on top of him, still seated, so she faced him straddling his waist.

As her heartbeat increased, she thought ever so briefly about running on the treadmill that afternoon and was glad that she had decided to come over.

CHAPTER 15

Silver got home from Dave's house late that night, and once again Anthony was already in bed. Her parents weren't coming home until tomorrow so there was no such thing as too late. Only, she made sure she was out of Dave's house before his mom came home.

Despite this new chapter in their relationship, she wasn't ready to meet his mom yet. And certainly not in the wee hours of the morning after she had spent the entire evening with her son. Alone.

She changed her clothes and got ready to go to bed, but she was in no mood to sleep. She still felt revved up.

Instead, she went over to her desk and sat down. She pulled a piece of paper out of the top right-hand drawer and began to read the words on it, committing it to memory. She knew it wouldn't take her very long. And she had until Wednesday anyway.

* * *

She sat at her desk in English and waited for Mr. Bailey to hand out the exams. It hadn't taken her very long to memorize the questions and answers she needed to know. She had it by the end of the day on Saturday. Now she sat here knowing exactly what to expect and what she needed to write.

As she looked around her classroom, the other students looked like the anticipation was killing them. No doubt they had been pouring over the exam review they had been given one week prior. They had probably done a lot of work. Technically, she had done a lot of work too. Just of a different nature.

Mr. Bailey stood up and without a word began walking down the rows of desks and handing each student a paper.

Silver was suddenly wrought with terror as she entertained the possibility that Mr. Bailey had decided to change the questions. Or that the questions had been different on each paper to begin with. She tried to remember if they had checked for that.

But regardless, the exam was now on her desk and there was nothing more she could do.

Silver looked down at it, and recognized all seven questions. She knew exactly what to do.

She happened to look up just as Mr. Bailey had finished handing out all the exams and noticed Anthony looking at her. He smiled and began work on his exam. She didn't want to look at the others, curious though she was, for fear of looking suspicious.

Silver began writing her first essay, moving quickly through all the points she knew should be there. Finally that one was finished and she moved on to the second and then the third, and not long after, all five essays were complete.

She read over her work, amazed it had been so easy. Well, easy during the exam, anyway, and realized that there was nothing more for her to do here. It appeared that she was the first one finished.

She thought about it and figured that it wouldn't be a good thing for her to be finished first. She would wait until someone else had already handed in the exam and then she would hand hers in.

She made herself look busy by changing a few words here and there.

As she heard the scraping of a chair on the floor, she knew that someone had finished. Good. Now she could turn in her exam and get out of here. But when she looked up at who it was, she wasn't very happy.

Anthony was walking toward Mr. Bailey's desk, papers in hand, his bag slung over his shoulder. He handed his exam, the exam questions (Mr. Bailey required these to be handed in with the finished exam), and his copy of the exam review (students who handed these back with their finished exams received an automatic extra 2 percent points on their exam) over to Mr. Bailey, who gave him a nod and a smile. Silver wondered what he must be thinking right now.

She definitely couldn't get up now; she'd have to wait for the next person.

Waiting like this was starting to make her anxious. She wanted to get out of here and get this all over with so she could move on with her life.

To her left, someone else was getting up. Karly.

Silver couldn't believe it. She should definitely have had a pre-exam discussion with everyone. It would have been different if Mike or Dave had gotten up first and second. But, Anthony and Karly, on the final exam? Dammit.

She kept on looking busy, practically boiling in her chair, waiting to see who would get up next and if she could hand in her exam.

A good ten minutes passed by before the next person, thankfully not Mike or Dave, got up to hand in their exam.

She couldn't wait any longer. She grabbed her bag and her exam papers and walked up to Mr. Bailey.

He looked at her and smiled as she handed it over.

She walked out of the classroom, unsure of whether this was over or not.

CHAPTER 16

Silver cornered Anthony in the cafeteria where he sat eating a package of chocolate covered donuts from the vending machine while waiting for his next class.

"Are you out of you mind?"

"What? I know the donuts aren't that healthy, but I'm hungry and I didn't get anything to eat before we left the house this morning."

"Not the donuts," she said dismissing the idea with a wave of her hand and sitting down across from him. "You were the first to," she lowered her voice, "turn in your exam. How many times this semester have you been first to turn in an exam?"

"But I was finished."

"You were finished because you cheated. This is what we don't want people to know."

"Silver, so what? So maybe I finally studied really hard and did well. He doesn't know anything just because I handed in my exam first and that's a little out of the ordinary."

Silver leaned across the table and her voice became a vicious whisper.

"He knows someone was in his house that night. Now, someone who barely has a C in the class has practically aced the exam."

Anthony looked at her like he was just remembering the night they almost got caught in Mr. Bailey's house.

"Well, I didn't write down all the answers. I skipped some of them."

"Did you write anything that wasn't on the answer key?"

"No."

Silver put her hand to her forehead and closed her eyes and tried not to scream at her brother. He popped a donut into his mouth and chewed slowly, watching her like she might explode right in front of him.

"Sorry," he said, looking a little sheepish.

This was her fault, she reminded herself. She should have been more clear about expectations for the exam. She assumed everybody knew what she did.

"It's all right," she said, some of the pressure she felt dispersing. "As long as you didn't write down every answer on that answer key, we're probably fine."

She got up to leave.

"Where are you going?"

"I'm going to go outside for a few minutes," she said, turning away and leaving Anthony to his donuts.

She prayed to God that Karly had been smart with her exam. That she hadn't written all the answers from the answer key. She was torn between wanting to go find out and not wanting to have anything more to do with her. Instead she exited from the side door and walked outside.

She could see her breath and it smelled a little bit like snow in the air. She wondered where Dave was. She wanted to talk to him.

She sat down at a picnic table that looked out over the grounds of the school and gazed off into the fields.

She couldn't seem to close this situation out. Just when she thought she had everything covered, something else happened that she hadn't predicted.

She wasn't sure exactly how Mr. Bailey could prove that they had cheated on the exams, but he had a decent lead with both Anthony and Karly finishing first and second, and their answers shockingly correct. She had the dreadful feeling that this was far from over.

And the graffiti. She hadn't heard anything much about this, but would Mr. Bailey connect the two together? If he could make a good case that they all cheated on the exam, he would have to tell the school administration about what had happened. No one in that office would be so foolish as to ignore the exceptional coincidence of that night.

She wanted to graduate right now. Get out of here, go to college and never have to look back.

"There you are," said a male voice.

She looked at Dave and half smiled, not because she wasn't glad to see him, but because she just didn't feel that good.

"Hey," she said, and scooted over on the bench making room for him next to her. "Did you just finish?"

"Actually, I finished one person after you. Well, I was finished before that, but you know, I was just waiting for the right time to get up."

"I wish Anthony and Karly had thought like that."

"Yeah, that was pretty stupid. But what's done is done."

She felt him reach down and grab her thigh, giving it a reassuring squeeze. It felt good, but if she was perfectly honest, she wasn't entirely comfortable with showing off their relationship in public. Sitting next to him here was okay, outside where no one was at the moment. But if someone saw him touch her, she wasn't sure how she felt about that.

She wanted to reach down and squeeze his hand back, but didn't. He pulled it away after a minute.

She had the thought that he was about to ask her "what's wrong?" And she was praying to God he wouldn't. She didn't feel like having that discussion when other things were on her mind right now.

"All right, I'm headed back inside."

He looked over at her like he was about to give her a quick kiss, but when she made no move toward him, he just got up and walked away.

As soon as he was gone, she wished he would come back.

* * *

Silver was walking to her next class when she heard someone call her name. She turned around and saw Jenna and Ashley, and was in no mood to talk to them.

"Hey," she said, hoping this conversation would go quickly. "What do you want?"

"I didn't know we had to specifically want something to talk to you," Ashley said.

"Sorry," Silver said, "I just had my English exam. Guess I'm not very cheerful right now."

Ashley sort of nodded in return, but didn't seem to actually believe her, but Jenna acted like she hadn't even noticed Silver's mood change.

"Do you want to come over this afternoon? Since we don't have practice today, we thought we all might just hang out," Jenna asked, sort of bouncing around on her feet like she did when she got excited.

"Uh ...," Silver started to say.

"Come on, a bunch of other people are coming too. My parents are gone this week so we'll have the house all to ourselves."

Silver didn't exactly know how to decline. Usually, she would have just been expected to be there, and she wouldn't have even thought of not going.

"Uh, I don't know. I was just going to go home. I'm kinda tired and frankly, haven't been feeling that well."

"What's going on with you?" Ashley asked. "Outside of practice, we've barely seen you the last few weeks. Are you making a bomb in your basement or something?"

"I don't know, I guess I've just been busy. I ... haven't been feeling like myself, lately."

This was actually the truth, and Silver felt no qualms about stating it. She really didn't want to go to Jenna's. In fact, she wasn't sure she wanted to hang out with them at all.

"All right, where's Anthony? Do you think he wants to come?" Jenna asked.

"Probably, and the last I saw him he was in the cafeteria shoving donuts in his mouth."

"Okay, well, text me if you want to come by."

"All right, I will."

The two girls walked away and Silver knew she had zero intention of going.

* * *

At home, Silver sat on her bed, her back up against the wall with her laptop across her thighs. She aimlessly surfed the web, reading little articles here and there, watching a couple of videos, and stalking her friends' online profiles.

She was now restless and bored.

She thought she had taken care of what was bothering her by apologizing to Dave. The night seemed to end well enough.

But something was bothering her again.

She closed the laptop and put it back on her desk and laid down on her bed with her eyes closed and her hands folded across her abdomen.

She had already gone running this afternoon, but she felt like she had more energy to burn again. At this rate, she should just train for a marathon.

Her phone beeped, and she figured it was Jenna or Ashley asking her if she wanted to come over again. Irritated, she picked up her phone, but saw that it was a text from Dave.

Where are you?

Hey, at home

Can i come over?

She was alone now, Anthony had gone over to Jenna's, and her parents wouldn't be home for several more hours, so she guessed it was okay. She didn't want Dave meeting her parents today.

Yeah, need my address?

She texted him her address and he said he'd be right over.

She lay back down again and started to think that maybe she was in over her head with this Dave thing.

The other night had happened so impulsively, she couldn't be sure that it was what she actually wanted. Although, she did want him to come over now; she didn't really feel like being alone.

She closed her eyes and the next thing she knew, her phone was beeping at her again.

Are you home? i tried knocking

Sorry, fell asleep, be right down

She got up from her bed feeling groggy and made her way downstairs to the front door. She opened it and there was Dave.

"Hey," he said, as she moved aside to let him in. He kissed her as he walked by. "What have you been doing?"

"Nothing, really. Napping, wasting time on the Internet."

"Where's your brother?"

"At Jenna's."

"Oh."

Dave went and sat down in the living room, motioning for her to join him. She walked to where he was on the couch and cuddled up beside him, enjoying the feeling of leaning up against his body. He draped an arm around her.

"So, you did it. It's all over," Dave said, looking over at her.

"Yeah," she said, not knowing what else to say. She sat there a moment trying to think of the words she wanted, but they never came to her. "No."

She pulled away from him and sat forward on the couch, putting her head into her hands.

"It's not over," she said. "That's not the feeling I get."

"What do you mean? Exam's over, Mr. Bailey is none the wiser."

'I don't know," she said, getting up and beginning to pace. "I might feel better when we all get our exams back and have our grades."

"But what kind of proof does he have that we cheated? The fact that our answers are similar isn't that odd."

"He's not a dumb man. Rigid, yes. Control freak, yes. But not dumb."

"I think you're worrying over nothing."

"I don't know," she felt like changing the subject. "Want a tour of the house?"

She assumed he answered yes because he stood up.

They walked around, looking at pictures here and there, her telling him little anecdotes about when she and Anthony were little and ducking into all the rooms to look around. Finally, they reached her bedroom.

"Let me guess, it's painted entirely in black and you have the heads of pigs on sticks stuck into the floor."

"You are really strange," she said as she walked in.

"I was thinking the same thing about you."

Silver's bedroom was small, but not tiny. The walls were painted blue, sky blue, and the furniture made it a little crowded. It was mostly neat, bed was made, no dirty dishes or anything like that, but there were some clothes lying on the floor and the tabletops were covered in stuff.

"Looks like a normal girl's bedroom," Dave said, as he walked around and looked at stuff.

"What were you expecting?"

"I told you already."

He walked over to the window and looked out.

"So this is it, this is my space."

She went over and sat on her bed, back against the wall, while Dave continued to look around. He picked up more pictures of her with her friends and studied them.

"Now that I know you, I can't figure out how you're a cheerleader."

"It's what I've always done," she said, shrugging. She enjoyed watching him handle all of her stuff. She remembered that she had done the same to him, he just didn't know that.

"Why don't you play basketball? Like Anthony."

"I don't know. I used to, but I stopped. I'm only average height, and wasn't that skilled otherwise to continue on with it."

Dave sat down in her desk chair and faced toward her.

"I feel like I'm seeing you from another angle. You may be a lot of things, but you're never boring."

"Do you like what you see?"

Dave just nodded.

"I feel like I could know you for another hundred years, and still not figure you out."

"You're trying to figure me out?"

"Maybe."

"You should stop doing that, eventually you'll find something you don't like."

Dave laughed, leaned back in the chair and rocked it back on two legs.

"If I haven't already found something that I dislike about you, I don't think I ever will. I don't think I've ever met anyone under stranger circumstances."

Silver laughed, and he looked right at her and smiled.

She scooted off the bed and walked toward him, sitting down on his lap without asking. His arm went around her waist and the other rested on her thigh.

She put a hand on his face and leaned in and kissed him, feeling the same energy from the other night return. Before she pulled away, she lightly bit down on his lower lip.

"You like to bite."

"I've never broken any skin," she said, and they both laughed.

"Do you really think this is going to be okay?" she asked.

He looked up at her.

"Yeah," he said, and she enjoyed the certainty in his voice.

"Do you feel bad?"

"A little bit, but if we ever get caught, I'll just tell him I did it for a girl. He'll understand."

CHAPTER 17

It was Wednesday. A week after they had taken the exam.

Silver walked into English anticipating the graded exams today. Mr. Bailey always returned exams a week later.

Once she had her graded exam in hand, this would all be over. She would have her grade, it would be in the books, and in a few weeks a new semester would begin and she wouldn't have to see Mr. Bailey anymore. She would be scot-free.

She sat down at her desk. Dave was already in his. He turned around to talk to her.

She felt weird again speaking to him in public, and she felt bad. She knew she shouldn't feel this way. She was fine with him in private. More than fine. But she still didn't like the idea of other people watching them interact.

Dave made small talk with her, telling her about some art project he was working on and asking her what she did last night. She noticed some people in the class lift their heads and look at them, watching them talk to each other.

One girl across the room turned to the girl next to her and whispered something.

Finally, Mr. Bailey walked in and Silver felt relieved on two accounts. She waited patiently for him to begin.

"Okay, class. I know I usually return exams after one week, but due to unforeseen circumstances, the grading has taken me a little longer. You will receive them back shortly, but I can't say exactly when."

Sounds of protest spread through the classroom. Everyone had expected them back today.

"I know, I know," Mr. Bailey waved his hands in a dismissive gesture. "Let's get started." He began to lecture.

Silver sat frozen in her seat, fear trickling out of every pore.

She wanted to catch Dave's eye, but didn't dare. Nor any of the others.

He knew. He definitely knew. And he was trying to figure out how to nail them.

Her ears were starting to ring, and her heart was racing. She stood up.

"I don't feel well. I've got to see the nurse."

She didn't wait for Mr. Bailey's reply. She stumbled out the door and into the hallway, starting to black out as she made her way to the nurse.

She made it, but just barely. The nurse took one look at her and had her lie down immediately. She then barraged Silver with a number of questions that all seemed to get at one thing. Was she pregnant? She could at least answer with certainty that she wasn't.

"I haven't been feeling well. I think I might be coming down with something," she told the nurse, who told her to lie down and be quiet for a while.

Anthony came in thirty seconds later. Mr. Bailey must have sent him after her.

"What's wrong?"

"I almost fainted."

"Are you feeling better?"

"Yeah," she said, telling the truth.

Anthony sat down on the edge of the cot and squeezed her shoulder.

"Do you need anything?"

"No, I'm just going to lie here for a while. I might go home, I guess."

"I can drive you if you need me to." He stood up, looked around for the nurse and lowered his voice. "I'm sure it's a coincidence."

"I don't know. He's always on time."

"You worry too much."

"That's what Dave said."

"Dave? You're still talking to him?"

She wanted to tell him the truth, but couldn't get it to come out of her mouth.

"Just when I run into him at school."

Anthony smiled and shook his head as he walked out of the room.

"You're too nice, Silver."

She laughed. That had to be a first.

* * *

"Hey, wait up!"

Someone behind her was trying to get her attention, and she knew exactly who it was.

Dave ran up beside her, and put a hand on her back. Silver sort of wriggled away, making it look like she was just changing positions.

"Are you all right? What happened?" Dave grabbed her arm to stop her from walking, which she really didn't want to do, but had no choice. "I've been trying to find you."

Silver put on her best casual face.

"Yeah, I'm fine. I got a little too warm. I think I might be coming down with something."

Dave looked at her like he was trying to figure out who this person was in front of him.

"You don't have to lie to me."

She didn't change her facial expression.

"No, it's fine. I'm fine. I left the nurse after an hour or so, and decided to go back to class."

Dave appraised her, trying to figure out what was really going on. He reached a hand out to her, but she pulled away.

"What's going on with you? You're like a different person right now. I know why you ran out of that classroom, Silver."

At that moment, Ashley walked by them and didn't do a good job of not staring. Silver made eye contact with her, but didn't wave or speak. She knew she'd be hearing from Ashley later.

Dave followed her eyes to where Ashley was, and looked back at her, having understood more than he was meant to.

"You don't want to be seen with me."

She didn't know what to say to him. She could have protested, but he would know that she was lying. He always knew things like that.

"Look, my friends, they—"

"Don't worry about it. I get it. But the next time you want someone to do your dirty work for you, call someone else."

He walked away from her down the hallway, disappearing into the crowd. The last thing she saw of him was the dragon on the back of his jacket.

Then, that disappeared too.

CHAPTER 18

Silver was a wreck. Over the last several days, she had only slept in fits and starts at night. She was jumpy and hostile during the days, and was only managing the most minimal interaction with other people.

She had spent the weekend practically locked in her room, or on the treadmill. She had probably spoken to Anthony twice, which was astonishing considering that they lived in the same house.

Thursday and Friday had gone by and still no graded exams. It was now Monday morning, and Silver wasn't sure how many days of this she could take. She thought that even sitting in jail would be better than this.

She arrived at school, dressed and mostly clean, but with no makeup on. She was sure the bags under her eyes made her look like some kind of an addict, but she couldn't bring herself to care. She was barely existing right now.

She and Dave acted like strangers to each other. Whatever it was they had, it was long gone. She couldn't tell if she was sad about that or not. She had the impulse to call him several times over the last few days, but each time she resisted. Probably because she knew he didn't want to hear from her, but maybe because she didn't want to feel like she wanted to talk to him. When Ashley had asked her about seeing them talking in the hallway, she had said that they had worked on a project together. And that's how she knew him.

She honestly didn't know how she was making it through the day. Around two o'clock, she had finally had enough. She didn't care if the police walked in and handcuffed her or if Mr. Bailey confronted her. She just wanted something to happen. Waiting like this had been a unique form of torture. She was ready for some action.

And that's exactly what she got.

She heard the sound that signaled a PA announcement and focused her attention on the message. They were calling her brother to the front office.

She told herself that maybe it wasn't what she thought. Maybe it was actually basketball related. Maybe the college he had committed to had left some kind of a message for him, or Coach Bryan wanted to talk to him or something. Maybe her parents had to speak with him.

She could have thought of all the excuses in the world, and not come up with one that made her feel better. This was it. It was starting.

She wanted to intercept him before he got to the office. He was in a classroom, just a couple doors down from her.

She got up quietly from her desk and left the room like she had to use the restroom.

She saw him in front of her a little ways down the hallway.

"Anthony!"

He turned around and looked surprised to see her.

"What are you doing?"

"Do you know what this is about?"

"No," she watched him swallow, "I thought it might be about basketball or something like that."

He was trying to do the same thing that she had been doing earlier. He didn't look like he really thought this was about basketball.

"I'm going to wait for you out here. Let me know what they say."

He nodded his head and swallowed again then continued on toward the front office.

Silver decided to take a walk around. It would look less suspicious than her just waiting around somewhere. She hoped this wouldn't take long. She couldn't stay out here forever.

She paced the hallways, making sure to walk neither too fast nor too slow. Just speedy enough to make it look like she was on her way to something, but not fast enough to make it look like she was in a rush.

She tried to calm herself down by running through all of the possible reasons Anthony could be needed in the office. It didn't make her feel better.

She walked around aimlessly, like a shark that needed to keep moving or would die.

Five minutes passed, then seven, eight, and finally it had been ten minutes since she left her classroom. She had to go back; she couldn't wait any longer.

She decided to swing by the office to see if she could see Anthony in there through the blinds, which she knew would be drawn, but which might be open a little.

She could never figure out why the front office had such large windows that faced into the school. Although she guessed that was what the blinds were for.

She strolled by the office, trying to see in between the slats, but didn't see Anthony at all.

She had no other choice but to head back. She'd see him after school anyways. She slipped back into her classroom and the teacher didn't even look at her, which was good since she had been gone so long. She sat there unable to focus on even the smallest thing, and did her best to wait for the class to be over.

When it was, she practically ran out the door.

She turned toward Anthony's classroom, practically pushing people out of the way as she went against the flow of foot traffic. Anthony was walking out just as she got there. She gestured to him "what happened."

"In the car," he said, turning swiftly in the direction of the exit.

They didn't speak until they were outside.

"How long were you in there?"

"About a half hour."

"Well?"

"I don't want to say anything until we're in the car."

Anthony walked up to the driver's side and Silver to the passenger's side. As the doors slammed shut, Silver launched into high gear, asking questions and barely allowing Anthony a word in edgewise.

"It's bad. They don't know for sure that I cheated, and I told them I just happened to finally study and get a few things right. But the principal was talking about a 'cheating ring.' They kept asking me things about who else might be involved. Not directly, but it was clear what they were getting at."

"Well, what did they ask? And who was there?"

"It was the principal and assistant principal. I can't quite remember all the questions. Just that there were some other exams in the class that were extremely similar to mine, and why did my answers match so well with those. And, you know, like did I usually finish exams early and what were my typical exam grades and stuff like that."

Silver leaned back in the seat and covered her eyes with her hand, wishing and praying that she had spoken to Anthony before the exam about not being obvious about having the answers. She could have prevented this.

"You should never have handed in your exam first. That was so obvious."

The vitriol in her voice was clear and it was also clear that she couldn't imagine a stupider move. When he spoke next, it almost sounded like his feelings were hurt.

"I know, but it's done now. I just ... you know, it felt good to be done and to know that I had practically aced it."

"Did they tell you what your grade was?"

He hesitated and she knew he didn't want to tell her what the answer was.

"They said I got an A."

Silver exploded. Days' worth of stress and anxiety shot out from her mouth as she let loose on her brother. When she was done screaming at him, they were almost home. She got out of the car, went into the house and immediately up to her room. Anthony didn't knock or try to come talk to her.

She lay there on her bed feeling her rapid heart rate and flushed cheeks. She couldn't believe how stupid he had been. Now there was some kind of evidence that cheating had occurred. She hadn't asked him if they had mentioned anyone else's names, and he hadn't said anything about that.

Of course, that might have been to avoid her anger and not because they didn't say anything.

She hoped that they didn't know everyone who was involved, but at this point, she knew that was too much to hope for. She resigned herself to the fact that she would be called up to the office soon too. Maybe even tomorrow.

* * *

The next morning, she still was only barely talking to Anthony, which was a little awkward considering that they drove to school together every morning. He seemed jumpy and overly concerned about staying out of her way. And that's how she liked it.

She had prepared herself overnight for today's imminent questioning, although luckily for her, it wasn't unusual for her to have aced an exam. Why her answers were so similar to four other exams in the class, however, she didn't have a good excuse for. She knew she'd think of something in the moment. She just hoped it happened early, so she wouldn't have to wait all day.

In English, they still hadn't gotten their graded exams back, which didn't surprise her at all. But the rest of the class was growing restless.

People had begun to talk about why they hadn't received their exams back, including a rumor that Mr. Bailey must have a terminal illness, but she hadn't heard anything about her situation, which was good. Everyone would know soon enough.

Silver was in Psychology before she heard the next PA announcement calling Mike to the office. Surely, Anthony had told him about his visit to the office yesterday. Mike must know what was coming.

She thought about fingerprints left behind in the lobby the night they had vandalized it, and then realized that dusting for prints might be a little much for graffiti in the school lobby. But maybe not. She had no idea.

Actually, what she hoped the most was that Mike wouldn't break down and confess. Of all of them, he was the most likely.

Silver stopped paying attention, and leaned back in her chair, and waited for her turn.

An hour or so later, she heard Karly's name called, and an hour or so after that, Dave's. She was next and she braced herself for it.

But she never heard her name called over the PA.

The final bell rung signaling the end of the day, and Silver had yet to visit with the principal. She couldn't figure out why.

She exited her classroom and was almost immediately accosted by Mike.

"We've all got to talk," he said, grabbing her upper arm as he did so and not letting her go.

"Okay, where are the others?"

"I'll get them. Where do you want to go?"

Silver thought about this, realizing that they couldn't meet anywhere in the school.

"The dugouts."

Mike nodded like that was a good idea and walked away.

The baseball field was away from the school a distance, and she didn't think anyone could see them if they were inside the dugouts. She grabbed her stuff and hurried outside.

She couldn't tell if it was just her mind playing tricks on her, but there seemed to be whispers and stares everywhere she went. Of course, after hearing all the PA announcements today, people must have started talking.

Silver pulled her coat around her tightly and looked over her shoulder once or twice as she headed out to the baseball field.

She sat down in the dugout, which kept out some of the wind, and waited. She hoped Dave wasn't the first one to come out.

She positioned herself so that she could see who was walking out of the building. She noticed Mike and Karly come out together.

When they were almost to her, Anthony walked out. Now they only waited for Dave.

Mike and Karly walked into the dugout and sat down on the bench, not really greeting her. She remembered that the last time she had spoken to Karly was in the parking lot when she had given her a copy of the exam. She had hoped not to have to deal with her again. Her wish had not come true.

Anthony came inside and sat down, breathing hard and looking a little flushed despite the cold air. He sat on the far end opposite of Silver, so that Karly was next to him, and Mike in between Karly and Silver.

At this point, she noticed Dave walk out of the building and her stomach fluttered. She watched him walk down to the field, his jacket buttoned up and his hands in his pockets, and felt an emotion she couldn't quite identify.

He finally walked in and sat down between Anthony and Karly.

"Why haven't you been called up?" Mike asked, turning toward Silver and putting his hands on his knees.

"I don't know," she said. "What did they say to you guys?"

"That our exams are similar. Also, apparently we all answered question #1 and no one else in the class did," Karly said. "But I don't understand. Yours must be similar too, so why haven't they gotten to you?"

"I don't know," Silver repeated as she leaned forward, thinking to herself that she had also answered question #1. "I was expecting to be next. What else did they say?"

"They asked me about the graffiti," Dave said, but not looking at her.

"Me too," Mike and Karly said at the same time.

"Me too," Anthony said, looking down at his feet and backing up further into the corner of the dugout.

He had withheld information from her, Silver thought, but she didn't have time to be angry.

"Did they mention anything about Mr. Bailey's house?"

"No," Mike said.

Silver was getting frustrated with her lack of information. She almost wished she had been called to the office because at least she would know what they were working with.

"Well, so, what are they going to do to you guys? How did it end?"

"Nothing really. Or nothing yet. I just tried to play it off like coincidence and that I didn't know anything about the graffiti or anything else. But they have to be connecting it together. Why else would they ask those questions?" Mike said.

Silver thought about what she had heard. The school administration obviously knew that these two events were connected, which meant Mr. Bailey had to have told them about his house being broken into. She looked up and noticed Karly shivering inside her coat, while looking down at the dirt at her feet.

Silver went back to her thoughts. But they obviously didn't quite have enough evidence to take any disciplinary action. She pondered once more why she hadn't been called to the office. And, suddenly, the answer was obvious. They didn't know her exam was also similar to these four. Mr. Bailey had never told them.

This didn't make any sense. If he had gotten this far with piecing together what had happened, he knew she was involved. The wind blew and she shivered inside her coat.

"Okay, well, I guess we wait."

"We wait?!" Mike jumped up. "Silver, I've got my whole future on the line. And not just that, but what about my dad?"

She wanted to tell Mike to grow a pair, but didn't think that would help the situation. And anyways, everyone here had participated willingly.

"I don't know what to tell you, Mike. But, clearly, they don't know enough to get you—us—for cheating and vandalism. We should just go about our business and let this thing blow over. It'll happen eventually."

Silver happened to look over at Karly, who kept looking up at her and then looking back down at the ground, her hands shoved into her coat pockets. Silver finally just looked at her and waited for her to speak.

"There is one more thing," Karly said, and Silver could tell that this would not be good news. "They found a ring in the lobby the night after. My ring."

The silence that reverberated around the dugout was one of the loudest sounds Silver had ever heard. It swallowed them all whole, and Silver waited for it to spit them back out.

"They don't know for certain that it's mine, and I didn't tell them it was."

"I told you not to wear any jewelry that night. There was a reason for that," Silver said, barely containing her anger. Mike's head was in his hands, and Dave and Anthony just stared at Karly wide eyed.

"I know, I just thought a little wouldn't hurt. The ring, it doesn't quite fit me, it slides around a lot on my finger. I didn't even realize it was gone until I was back home that night. Guys, I'm sorry."

"They don't know for sure that it's yours," Dave said, and Silver found herself admiring his kindness, even though she now thought Karly was not only the most annoying, but the stupidest person in the world.

Finally, Silver had had enough. She began to tell Karly exactly what she thought about her ring-wearing during that night, adding in enough expletives to let her know that she was serious. Even though her voice was even, the anger in it was enough to practically set the dugout on fire. If she hadn't known better, she would have sworn that the steam from their breathing was actually the wood beginning to smoke.

"Silver, that's enough."

It was Anthony. He had sat a little forward and was looking directly at her. She looked up in surprise from her diatribe.

"This is just one mistake out of many. And, frankly, you're not even in the same position we're all in now. If this is the straw that broke the camel's back, we go down with it, not you."

Silver knew that there were words forming in her brain, but for some reason they were not making their way to her mouth. She suddenly didn't feel in charge any more.

"There's always tomorrow," she said. "Maybe they couldn't get to me today."

"Maybe," Anthony said, then leaned his head up against the wall.

"So what happens now?" Dave asked.

Normally, Silver would have answered this, but given the circumstances and the speaker, she felt it was someone else's to give.

"There's nothing to do," Anthony said. "We wait. Without a confession or more direct evidence, they don't have anything on us."

Anthony got up, and then Mike, Dave, and Karly. The latter three exited the dugout without a word.

"You coming? I'll be at the car," Anthony said, and he too left the dugout.

Silver sat there a moment watching the steam from her breath, and wondering at which point this all got away from her.

CHAPTER 19

They were finally getting their exams back. Two weeks after they had taken them.

Silver held hers and looked at the big blue A on the top of it. She flipped through, but the rest of the exam was clean. No notes, no marks, no comments. It didn't feel as good to her as she thought it would.

She guessed that she would be moving forward with her plans now. That everything would fall into place just as she wanted it to. It was funny though, with all of the activity of the last month, she hadn't really been thinking much about her future, and suddenly the plans that had been so important to her seemed like a distant memory. The time passing had made them a little fuzzy. She guessed she should be happy.

She grabbed her bag and pulled out a pack of gum, opened a piece and popped it into her mouth. She crumpled up the wrapper and walked to the trash can by Mr. Bailey's desk. She happened to look up at his computer screen as she walked by and noticed that it was open to what looked like pictures of students. Maybe photos for the yearbook or something. She made a mental note then quickly let it go, thinking that maybe Mr. Bailey was the advisor for the yearbook.

She sat back down and people were still mulling over their exams, some moaning about their grades or about little comments made here and there.

She noticed that Dave had opened up his book and was reading, his exam laying on his desk with a big blue A on top also. But she knew that he would have gotten that anyway.

* * *

The next few days went by. School, cheer practice, a basketball game, and then it was time for the Winter Break.

Silver spent it quietly and reclusively. She actually started to wish that she liked to read like Dave did. That would pass the time.

She stayed in her room and remembered the afternoon she had Dave up here, actually touching her stuff and sitting in her chair. That felt like a really long time ago, although only weeks had passed.

This didn't feel at all like she thought it should. She waited to go back to school.

Something had changed between her and Anthony, but she couldn't quite put a finger on it.

He didn't come knock on the door to her room, and she didn't barge into his, so they could hang around and talk about nothing. They spoke to each other, but politely, formally even, and he didn't seem as interested in what she was doing or how she was feeling. She felt like she didn't even know him that well.

Finally, they were back at school and a new semester had started. Things had quieted down, and there was no more mention of cheating or vandalism. She guessed that the school administration just didn't have enough on them and had let the whole thing go. They were free.

In the first few days of the semester, she barely saw any of the other four. She did have one class with Mike, but aside from greeting each other, they didn't really talk.

Basketball season was now in high gear, so there were a couple of games each week, which kept Silver busy, but she just went through the motions. She started to wonder if she had ever really liked doing this.

Silver wandered through her daily activities. Always busy, but not feeling much of anything. She vaguely wondered when it would stop.

She hadn't seen Dave at all, and she hadn't gone looking for him. Nor him for her. The art case had been switched up and his ceramic dragon was no longer there. She wondered how he was, and was glad, especially for his sake, that they hadn't gotten caught. He would have taken a pretty big fall. She felt a little ashamed that she had asked him to do it.

Silver settled in for the semester, waited for graduation, and felt little emotion about it. She just wanted it to be over.

About a week after school resumed, Silver went to school feeling strange. She had woken up that morning and didn't feel right. Nothing specific had happened, there was just something in the air.

She felt unbalanced all day, as if she walked more heavily on one side of her body than the other. It made her uneasy.

When she heard the PA announcement calling Karly to the front office, she perked up for just a minute, then rationalized to herself that it must be for some random reason. But, nonetheless, her mind wouldn't let go of it.

A little later, she thought about it again, and wondered what it had been for.

A little later after that, she heard the PA again, and this time it called Dave, Mike, and her brother all at once. Now she knew exactly what this was about, but it seemed impossible to her that this was happening now. They had gotten away with this.

She would have gotten up and left her classroom, but she knew that they wouldn't be finished yet. It had barely begun. This time she didn't wait for her name to be called. She knew it wouldn't.

When class ended, she got up slowly, in no rush to confront what had happened and walked up toward the front office.

Her first sign that something was horribly wrong was the sight of her parents walking through the hallway and exiting through the lobby. She made sure that they didn't see her. She saw Anthony next, exiting the front office. He saw her and the expression on his face was a mixture of shock and shame.

"I've been suspended. We all have. We might not be able to graduate."

Silver didn't know what to say, and before she could think of anything, Anthony walked away, following her parents out of the lobby.

She watched as Mike's dad walked in next, passing her brother and not saying a word. He reminded her of one of those cartoons where smoke comes out of the character's ears.

She turned away and walked back in the direction she had come, wanting to get away from Mike's dad and anyone else that she might run into.

She had to get out of here. She couldn't go home, but she could go somewhere else. She'd figure that out once she got in the car.

She hadn't even asked Anthony how the school administration had figured it out. What else they had found. She had forgotten about that in the moment. She knew she'd find out soon enough.

She walked to her locker to grab her stuff so she could leave, but as she approached, she was dismayed to find something taped to the outside of it.

As she got closer she realized it was a photograph. She took the photo in her hands and yanked it off her locker where it had been affixed with some tape.

In the picture were three girls. She didn't recognize any of them at first, but she noticed that they were definitely inside the school. It looked like the kind of photo that would go into the yearbook. Then she noticed that the middle girl was Karly.

Karly stood with her arms around each friend's shoulders so that both of her hands hung close to their necks.

It was then Silver noticed the pen mark on the photo circling Karly's right hand and the ring she wore on her middle finger.

Silver recognized that ring. She had seen Karly wear it dozens of times, including the night they stole the exam. It was clunky and silver and had a large green stone in the middle of it. It hung on her finger off to one side, like it didn't fit her that well.

And to think, she had been more worried about the bracelets.

CHAPTER 20

Silver knew right then what she needed to do. She just needed to prepare herself for it. The thing she had been looking for to set things right, this was it. She was absolutely certain of it. Unfortunately.

She left school and drove aimlessly, then got some coffee at a café and sat there for a bit. She couldn't go home until school was over, otherwise her parents would know that she had skipped.

She'd miss cheer practice too. Oh well. She wouldn't be on the team much longer anyway. Ashley could take over. She'd make a decent captain, and Silver knew she wanted it.

In the middle of the afternoon, she started home, and even though she wasn't the one in trouble, she shuddered at what she might find there.

She opened the door to her house and the anger floated palpably through the air. She didn't see anyone, though. For a second, she wondered where everyone was, then sprinted up the stairs to get to her room before she found out.

She thought about the other three and wondered what was happening to them. She hoped that Mike was okay.

Silver sat down at her laptop, pulled up a blank document and began writing. As she put the words on paper, relief washed over her, even as she knew what lay ahead. Once outside of her brain, they were no longer just her burden, and she wished that she had done this a long time ago. She now felt light, where she had always felt dense, and despite what would happen next, everything would be okay in the end.

She finished what she was writing and hit the print button, ready to set things right. What she should have done from the beginning. Only she hadn't known. She hadn't known until now.

* * *

She walked into school early the next morning before anyone was there. Today it had been easy to come early since Anthony wasn't going to school. She brought what she had written last night, as well as a copy of the exam with the answers.

She moved with purpose through the hallways, not stopping to do anything, but in front of his door she stopped. For just a second she hesitated, then gathered up all her energy and before she could think too much, burst through Mr. Bailey's mostly shut classroom door.

She swore that when he looked up at her he had just the faintest trace of a smile on his face.

"Yes, Silver? You're here early."

"Mr. Bailey, I have something I need to tell you."

Silver walked in the rest of the way and shut the door behind her.

CHAPTER 21

Silver walked up to Dave's house and knocked on the door. She had decided recently that it was time to do this. She hadn't let him know she was coming. Partly because they hadn't spoken to each other in months.

It was late on a Saturday afternoon, and even though there was a decent possibility that his mom was there, Silver still decided to go over anyway. It just felt like the right time.

The weather had warmed up. No more coats and sweaters. Silver's arms were bare and the sun and the breeze touched them in a way that made her feel peaceful and safe. She waited for someone to open the door.

Out of the corner of her eye, she thought she saw someone peek around the curtains quickly then disappear. There was a possibility that he wouldn't open the door for her. She knew that.

But a second later, she heard the lock move and another second later Dave stood in front of her in a white T-shirt.

He looked at her like he was seeing a ghost.

"Hi," she said.

"Hi." He didn't move from the door frame. "What are you doing here?"

"I wanted to talk to you."

He seemed to be considering whether this was a good idea or not. Finally, he shrugged his shoulders.

"Okay, come on in." He stepped aside and allowed her into his house.

Silver felt fully familiar with this place, and she realized that she had missed it. It was quiet inside, with the late afternoon sunlight streaming in through the windows. There was noise coming from one of the bedrooms. She guessed his mom was home.

Dave gestured toward the couch and Silver sat down. Dave sat on the other end. Déjà vu.

"I'm surprised you let me in," she said.

"I prefer not to hold grudges."

"Very noble of you."

"It's not noble. It's practical. And, I can't say I'm not curious about what you have to say."

"I hate to disappoint you. It's nothing specific, I just felt the urge to come see you." She looked at him directly then and felt that pull. She wasn't able to read him very well right now. "So what's been going on?"

Dave crossed his ankle over one of his knees and draped his arm across the back of the couch. His arm looked different. The muscle definition was more apparent, and the shape of his arm was different.

"Your arm is different," she said before he had a chance to answer her question. "What have you been doing?"

"Lifting," Dave said, as he nodded his head over to a corner of the house where Silver could see a bench press, some weights stacked up and some dumbbells. "There's no room for it in the house. I move it into the kitchen when I want to use it."

Silver had the sudden urge to ask him to take off his shirt so she could see the full results, but thought to herself that this was not the appropriate time.

"Cool," she said. "What else is new?"

Just then, the noise from the bedroom stopped and Silver heard footsteps in the hallway. She got nervous.

A woman, who she could only assume was Dave's mom, stepped out from the hallway. She was dressed in black and her hair was pulled back. Silver assumed she was going to work. She waited to be spoken to first, as she hadn't exactly prepared herself for this.

Dave's mom looked at her, then at Dave and raised her eyebrow.

"Mom, this is Silver."

Dave's mom looked at her, then, and to Silver's relief, actually smiled. In fact, she appeared quite amused.

"So this is the Bonnie to your Clyde. Hi Silver, I'm Jeannie." Jeannie walked toward her and held out her hand to her. Silver got up and met her, taking her hand in a comfortable handshake.

"That's me," she said feeling a little sheepish, but pleasantly surprised that his mom seemed so friendly. "Nice to meet you."

Jeannie was probably seven or eight years younger than her parents, Silver thought.

"I've got to go," Jeannie said to Dave, as she walked over to him and kissed him on top of the head. She grabbed a bag off the table, and opened the door. "Bye, guys."

"Bye, Mom," Dave called out as she exited the house.

"Your mom was shockingly friendly to me."

"What were you expecting?"

"Well," Silver walked back over to the couch and sat down, "considering I almost got you, myself, and three others expelled in the middle of our senior year, I was expecting her to not be so cheerful upon meeting me."

Dave gestured with his hands that this was all water under the bridge.

"It all worked out in the end, didn't it? None of us got expelled, we'll all graduate, and for me, at least, there wasn't really anything they could kick me out of. Putting me out of the art club just doesn't have the same ring to it as getting kicked off the basketball team. Or off the cheer squad."

Silver nodded her head and rolled her eyes at this, but smiled too.

"Yep, that is correct," she paused a moment, thinking, "but you know what? It wasn't really that bad. After a few weeks, I got used to it, and then, it just seemed normal. Like I was never a part of it to begin with."

"Funny you say that. I ran into Mike a few weeks ago, and he kind of said the same thing. I asked him how he was doing and he said, 'relieved.' Actually, you should see what he made in ceramics this semester. It's this castle, and it's huge. And really detailed. It's awesome. Actually, I think it's in the case."

"I think I've seen it," Silver said, and then added, "His hair is really getting long."

"I know. It's pretty crazy. What about your brother?"

"Well, he won't be playing basketball in college like he thought," Silver smiled here again, but in a guilty way. She still felt really bad about this. "But he is still going to the same school. He thinks he might be able to play on a club team or something. But you know Anthony, it's already kind of rolled off him. He's just moving forward with whatever he's got."

"And what about you? What's going on with you?"

"Well, I got a job," she said, and was amused at Dave's surprise. "I'm paying back all the expenses for the damages, so I still haven't seen a penny of it."

"You know, I'd love to watch you do honest work. That must be a sight to behold," he laughed at her in spite of himself.

Silver laughed too.

"Is that all?" Dave asked.

"No," Silver remembered the other thing that was keeping her busy nowadays, "I'm actually training for a marathon. Since I pretty much got kicked out of every club and activity I had been a part of, you know, that really freed up a lot of my time."

Dave threw his head back at this and laughed. Silver didn't think she had ever seen him so expressive and was amused at how much he had let go.

"It's true," she said. "I show up at school and I go home."

"Flew a little too close to the sun, huh?"

Silver chuckled as she nodded in agreement.

"What about school next year?"

This one still hurt to say, but she was getting used to it.

"Community college. And I'm paying for it."

Dave raised his eyebrows, but didn't laugh at this one, knowing that this was the part that stung the most.

"I am too," he said. "But that was always my plan."

He sat there a moment, staring at her with a thoughtful expression on his face.

"Are you trying to figure me out again?" Silver said and smiled.

"I was just thinking ... you were always trying to get everything, and ended up with nothing. You never ended up getting what you wanted."

Silver considered this.

"I'm not so sure that's true," she said, and left it at that. Dave didn't ask any more questions. She noticed his face light up.

"You know what? I have something to show you."

He got up and started walking back toward the bedrooms, motioning for her to follow him. She followed him into his room, and it was just the way she remembered it, complete with unmade, but sort of made, bed.

He walked over to a stack of canvases leaning against the wall, and picked one up, being careful not to expose it to her.

He sat down on his bed and motioned for her to sit next to him.

"This is something I just finished not too long ago."

She sat down next to him and took in the painting. It was of a silver dragon.

The dragon's body was narrow and slender, winding its way toward the top of the page. It had the appearance of being metallic in places, cool, hard, and shiny, and in other places softer and curvy. Dave had designed it with something like a mane around its neck. It appeared to be in flight, with a bluish, greenish, grayish background that suggested the sky.

"Very subtle," she looked over at him and couldn't help but smile.

"What? It's just something I made. Thought you'd be interested. You seem to always like my dragons." He smiled back.

"Well, at least it's not breathing fire on a village full of innocent people."

"Nah, it has more open space now. Even if it did breath fire, it wouldn't hit anything."

"It's really cool," she said and meant it. She studied the painting a little longer and admired the detail work then looked up at him. "You know, I would be totally willing to humble myself and ask you, again, to go to prom, except that I've been banned from attending."

"What a coincidence. I've been banned too."

The two of them laughed at this as if it was the funniest thing they had ever heard.

"Serves us right, doesn't it?" Dave said.

"Yeah, I guess," Silver paused. "But if you still wanted to, we should go out and do something. Like a non-prom, prom."

She waited for him to respond, not knowing which way this would go.

"What about tonight?" he said.

"Really?"

"Yeah, absolutely."

"Okay, sure."

"Actually, let's leave right now. I'm hungry."

"All right, let's go."

She didn't move to get up, and he looked at her with a worried expression.

"I really wasn't sure you would ever want to speak to me again, much less let me inside your house and hang out."

His gaze never left her face.

"I told you, I don't like holding grudges. And ..." she waited for what he would say next. "You keep things exciting."

She smiled and he smiled even wider.

"That's a nice way of saying it."

She got up from the bed and he got up too.

"So where are we go—"

"Wait a minute," he interrupted her, "I've got one more thing to show you. You'll really love this."

Silver was intrigued; she wasn't sure what could top the silver dragon. Dave moved around her to walk ahead into the hallway. He walked toward a closet door located near the entrance of the house and opened it.

Silver watched the muscles in his arm flex as he reached in and pulled out a black leather jacket.

"Look what I found." He put it on and it looked great on him.

"What do you mean 'found'?" Silver asked.

"In a thrift store. I bought it in a thrift store. I had to dig around for a while, but I saw this and it was exactly my size. I figured it had to be a sign."

She looked at him and thought he might be teasing her.

"So this means you've thrown away or burned the denim jacket, right?"

"Oh no," Dave reached back into the closet and pulled on the sleeve of the denim jacket so Silver could see it. "That's staying right here for safekeeping. You never know when I might need it again."

Just then, Silver glanced at the key hook, and noticed a lone key strung through a piece of leather. She walked over and handled it, letting it fall back into place. It made a sound as it hit the other keys.

"I'm really sorry I put you in that position with Mr. Bailey," she said, worried that she had completely ruined their relationship.

"It's okay. Really," Dave said, and walked toward the key himself. "I walked over there one day, apologized, gave him all the details he wanted—he was actually very curious—and we decided that from now on, I would feed his cats free of charge. I've also become the lawn boy—also free of charge—for anything he needs done."

"Does that involve taking off your shirt?" Silver asked, putting her hand on his arm and shamelessly feeling how muscular he had gotten.

"It hasn't been that warm yet, but you never know," Dave said smiling, as he put the leather jacket back into the closet. "Ready?"

Silver nodded. They both moved to walk out the door, but Silver stopped.

"It's funny," she said, "this feels like the end, but I actually think it's the beginning."

Dave looked at her, keys in hand, with a faint smile on his face. "Is there any difference?"

The End

JOIN MY NEWSLETTER AND RECEIVE THE SOMMER HOUSE FOR FREE

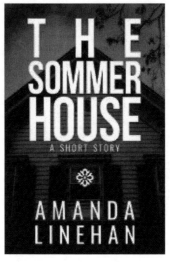

Join my newsletter and get a free, exclusive copy of *The Sommer House*, a YA horror short story. It's not published anywhere else and is about 5,000 words (roughly a 25 minute read.)

I send a newsletter once a month on the 3rd Tuesday, and every once in a while a second email during the month. Inside every newsletter there are updates on my current fiction projects, any promotions/discounts/giveaways/freebies I've got going on, blog posts I've written recently and a free short story (under 1,000 words so it can be read in about five minutes). You can unsubscribe at any time.

Sign up here: amandalinehan.com/newsletter[1]

---

1.   http://amandalinehan.com/newsletter/

Did you love *The Test*? Then you should read *North* by Amanda Linehan!

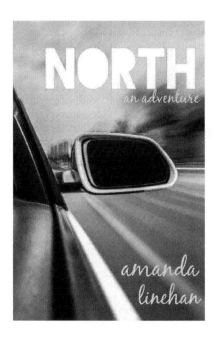

Jayne is on the run. With a bag full of stolen money, a new friend she met while stealing his car, and an old adversary out to get her, Jayne heads north looking for a better life.Along the way she encounters adventure, danger, freedom and something she never expected — love.But before she can reach her destination she must confront something that's been following her all along. When she least expects it, her past collides with her future and she must decide whether to keep running or return home to rebuild the life she left.

Read more at amandalinehan.com.

Also by Amanda Linehan

Watch for more at amandalinehan.com.

About the Author

Amanda Linehan is a fiction writer, indie author and INFP. She has published five novels, six short stories and two short story collections. Her stories have been read by readers in 86 countries. Amanda has been self publishing since 2012. Her short fiction has been published in *Every Day Fiction* and in the *Beach Life* anthology published by Cat & Mouse Press. She lives in Maryland, likes to be outside and writes with her cat sleeping on the floor beside her desk.Contact Amanda by email: amanda@amandaline-han.com, on Twitter: @amandalinehan or on her website: aman-dalinehan.com.

Read more at amandalinehan.com.

Made in the USA
San Bernardino, CA
21 July 2020